Outrageous Exposures

Within the space of a few weeks one October three young women disappeared in and around Oxford. All they had in common were good looks and long hair.

In his latest crime novel John Penn introduces a new member of the Thames Valley Police Force —Detective Chief Inspector Dick Tansey—who with a woman sergeant is given the unwelcome task of investigating this sequence of events. Soon, however, it becomes clear that there is a great deal more to the case than the almost routine abduction of young girls. Murder follows murder, an ex-convict is involved, the secret lives of the victims prove important, the relationship between Tansey and his sergeant develops, and disturbing but rarely explored facets of human character are revealed.

This book is a new departure for John Penn—a far cry from the eight classic crime stories he has written in the past. His many fans will enjoy it for its complexity, characterization and humanity.

JOHN PENN

Outrageous
Exposures

COLLINS, 8 GRAFTON STREET, LONDON W1

William Collins Sons & Co. Ltd
London · Glasgow · Sydney · Auckland
Toronto · Johannesburg

First published 1988
© John Penn 1988

British Library Cataloguing in Publication Data

Penn, John
    Outrageous exposures.—(Crime club)
    I. Title
    823'.914[F]

ISBN 0 00 232208 0

Photoset in Linotron Baskerville by
Rowland Phototypesetting Ltd
Bury St Edmunds, Suffolk
Printed in Great Britain by
Mackays of Chatham PLC, Letchworth.

CHAPTER 1

Kate Minden was the first—the first of the young women who disappeared in and around Oxford within the space of a few weeks in October.

Kate Minden was twenty-seven, an attractive woman with beautiful long red hair, who for eighteen months had been the sole secretary at a small estate agency in Kidlington, a northern suburb of the city. She was a good worker, with excellent skills and a pleasant telephone manner. She was often alone in the agency when customers called, because both the senior partner, Tony Knight, and his junior, Peter Cousin—the only two other members of the firm—naturally spent a great deal of their time out and about, inspecting properties or escorting prospective clients. Kate dealt with casual drop-in customers admirably, and was, in short, an ideal secretary for such a firm.

Tony Knight, a cheerful man in his early forties, who was struggling hard to make the business a success, was fully appreciative of Kate's qualities. From his point of view his secretary had only one drawback. When she was first interviewed for the post, she had made a single stipulation. During the week she would work long hours whenever overtime was required, without expecting any addition to a salary that no one could call generous. But she would not work after four-thirty on Friday afternoons, or at any time during weekends, however pressing the need.

Knight had agreed to this condition readily enough, although Saturday was often his busiest day. At the money he was offering he had scarcely hoped to find a secretary with Kate's qualifications and experience, and he didn't inquire about her reasons for leaving her last job, with a computer firm in Reading. It was enough for Knight that her previous employers had been reluctant to let her go, and had provided excellent references.

And during the time she had been with the firm, Knight had never had occasion to regret his decision. Kate's stipulation about weekend work had been inconvenient, admittedly, but his daughter came in after school on Fridays, mainly to answer the telephone, and his wife, who had at first been reluctant, now admitted to enjoying a Saturday shift in the office. Of course, the arrangement was not ideal —one sale had been lost as a result of his wife muddling an appointment—but on the whole it worked well.

There was nothing unusual about Kate's last Friday with A. J. Knight's Estate Agency. She arrived punctually in the morning, as always on Fridays carrying a small overnight case. She had a key to the front door, and as usual found Knight already at work. He lived with his family in the maisonette above the office, and liked to get an early start on the paperwork before the real business of the day began. For him, this was selling houses. He positively enjoyed what he described as fitting the right property to the right person or persons. Inevitably, he had been glad to leave more and more of the routine office work to Kate.

Kate's own desk was in the main office—a showroom of moderate size, lined with screens showing photographs of a variety of more or less desirable properties. Two display windows, also with screens of photographs, flanked the main street door to the premises.

Kate left her overnight case beside her desk, put her handbag in a drawer and at once went through to the smaller room behind, which was shared by the two partners. For almost an hour she worked together with Knight, checking appointments, sorting photographs, considering potential clients and their mortgages and problems, and planning the week ahead. They scarcely looked up when Peter Cousin came in.

Cousin, the junior partner, was a younger man than

Knight—about Kate's age. He was attractive in an ugly kind of way, but no one could have persuaded him of this fact. He had been born with one leg slightly shorter than the other, so that he limped as he walked; he was sure that every woman who smiled at him was merely showing pity for this slight infirmity. But this feeling had not prevented him from falling hopelessly in love with Kate, though his innate inferiority complex had always prevented him from making any approach to her.

'A very good morning to you both,' he said with exaggerated cheerfulness. 'I've news for you, and I expect some congratulations.'

'You haven't got yourself engaged at last?' Knight suggested jovially.

'No,' Cousin said shortly. There was a distinct pause before he went on less excitedly. 'But I've pulled off that Dorland deal.' He opened his briefcase and produced a sheaf of papers. 'Here it is. All signed and sealed, and no strings attached or snags that I can see.'

'That's splendid!' Kate said at once. 'Congratulations indeed, Peter.'

'I'll buy you a drink when we close up tonight,' Knight promised, taking the papers. He was equally pleased; this was a big sale which would help to reduce the firm's overdraft considerably. 'Well done, Peter.'

'Thanks. I'm pretty chuffed about it myself,' Cousin admitted. 'I'll be asking for a rise soon. Meanwhile I'll settle for that drink, Tony—but not tonight. I've got a deal going over in Cowley. It's a double. You know, they'll buy if they can sell, and I think I've found a buyer for them.'

'Good!' Knight's attention had returned to the work in front of him.

On his way through the showroom Cousin had noticed Kate's overnight bag beside her chair. He said to her, 'If you're off for your usual dirty weekend tonight, Kate, I can

give you a lift into central Oxford. I'll be leaving aound
four-thirty.'

'Okay, Peter. Many thanks.'

Kate smiled her gratitude. It had become an office joke
that Kate spent every weekend with a boyfriend in Reading,
which was why she insisted on leaving early on Fridays. She
had never made the slightest attempt to confirm or deny the
story. Her private life, she implied very clearly, was her
own.

'Great! My pleasure,' said Cousin. 'I've got to drive over
to Burford this afternoon to photograph a property, but I'll
be back in plenty of time, so not to worry. That reminds me
—I'm completely out of film. I must get some before I go,
or I'll not be able to do my Lord Snowdon act.'

The reference was stale from repetition, and failed to raise
a laugh. But in fact Cousin was an excellent photographer.
All the prints on display in the windows and on the walls
of the agency were his work, and his boast—that he could
make any property look worth twenty-five per cent more
than its true value—was fully justified.

'Actually, I think I'll go and get some right away.' Cousin
made for the door.

'Buy some stamps at the same time. We're getting low,'
Knight said.

'Will do.' With a wave of his hand Cousin left them.

A young couple, who had been staring at the photographs
in the windows, came somewhat doubtfully into the shop.
Tony Knight put on his most avuncular manner, and went
forward to ask how he could help them. The telephone rang,
and Kate answered it.

A new day had begun. There was nothing to indicate that
it would be Kate Minden's last at A. J. Knight's Estate
Agency.

The day was a busy one. For most of the time Kate was
alone in the office, though this held no worries for her.

Between answering the phone, making appointments for clients to view, preparing data sheets for various properties and dealing with the casual caller who came in off the street, she was too occupied to think much about the weekend ahead. But occasionally she remembered, and she smiled happily to herself.

As usual, she worked through most of the lunch period. At the rear of the premises, next to the washroom, was a small kitchen with a gas ring and facilities to make a hot drink to go with the sandwiches and fruit she had brought. She put a 'Closed' notice on the door, and for twenty minutes settled down to eat in the partners' office, a book propped up on Knight's desk in front of her. Nevertheless, she did answer the telephone, which rang twice during this time with routine inquiries.

As the afternoon drew on, she began to feel impatient, and found herself resisting a temptation constantly to consult her watch or look at the office clock. Tony Knight came in for a while, then went out again.

'Well, I had a wasted morning,' he remarked as he departed. 'Damned client looked over that house for a third time, and then decided it didn't get enough sun.' He shook his head sadly at the vagaries of house buyers. 'Let's hope this next effort'll produce more fruit—and bread for the firm.' He grinned.

'Good luck,' Kate said. 'I'll see you on Monday, Tony. Have a nice weekend.'

'You too, Kate. 'Bye for now.'

At ten minutes past four Kate went to the lavatory, washed her hands, ran a comb through her hair and re-touched her make-up. When she returned to the office she found Peter Cousin sitting on a corner of her desk.

'Car waiting at the door, madam.'

'Thanks, Peter, but I can't go yet—not for another quarter of an hour, not till Diana arrives. But if you want to—'

'No. I'm in no hurry.'

Kate started typing a letter Knight had dictated during his brief visit, and Cousin began leafing through one of the agency's portfolios of property photographs. But by twenty-five past four Kate was becoming anxious; Diana, Tony Knight's daughter, had not yet appeared.

The girl came into the shop precisely on the half-hour, and listened sulkily to the brief instructions Kate had to give her. Diana Knight was fifteen, and passing through the traditionally 'difficult' stage. In her case it manifested itself by a scarcely concealed hatred of everyone and everything. Short and inclined to plumpness, she particularly envied and resented Kate's slim elegance and apparent sophistication. She merely grunted when Kate wished her a good weekend, but she went to the door, and watched Cousin help Kate into the car before they drove off together.

The telephone was ringing and, as Diana went to answer it, she glanced at her watch. The time was twenty-two minutes to five.

On the following Monday morning Kate Minden failed to appear at the offices of A. J. Knight's Estate Agency in Kidlington.

'She must have missed her bus,' Cousin said.

Fortunately business was not heavy, and Knight was able to rearrange his appointments so that he had no need to leave the office immediately. He expected Kate to arrive at any moment, full of apologies. But when she hadn't arrived by noon, and there had been no news of her, he became angry.

'What the hell can have happened to the girl?' he demanded of Cousin, who had returned from a morning showing houses. 'She could have caught half a dozen buses by now. Or if she's ill, or her boyfriend's ill, or something's prevented her from coming in, why hasn't she phoned? It's most unlike her. She's always been so reliable in the past,' he ended plaintively.

'Perhaps her phone's out of order, and she can't get to another,' Cousin suggested. 'Anyway, I expect there's a simple explanation, so don't worry, Tony. She'll turn up.'

'I damn well hope so, or we'll have to get in a temp.'

'Don't start thinking about that yet, Tony. Give Kate a chance. Meanwhile, what about that drink you promised me on Friday? Surely we can shut this place up for half an hour.'

Rather reluctantly Tony Knight agreed, and the two men were on the point of leaving for their nearest pub—only a few doors away along the street—when the telephone rang. Knight seized the receiver.

'Knight's Estate Agency,' he said. He frowned. 'Who? Oh, you mean Kate. No, I'm sorry, but she's not in today. No, I don't know. Can I take a message? Yes. Yes. I've got that.' He scribbled a number on a memo pad. 'And your name?' He paused for a moment, then replaced the receiver and stared at Cousin. 'That's odd. She just cut me off.'

'What was it all about?'

'A woman—she sounded a bit nervous—wanted to speak to Mrs Katerina Minden.'

'Our Kate? Mrs?'

'That's what she said. She left a phone number and a message asking that Kate should call her urgently. But she wouldn't leave a name.'

'Odd indeed! Are you sure you didn't misunderstand her, Tony? About the "Mrs", I mean.'

'Quite sure! But, as I said, she sounded kind of nervous, so she could have made a mistake.' Knight hesitated. 'You don't think Kate could be married to this mysterious boyfriend of hers, do you, Peter?'

'Noo—o,' said Cousin slowly. 'I don't know, but somehow I doubt it.' He shrugged. 'And where was the call from? Reading?'

'No. That's another oddity. The code shows the woman

was calling from Abingdon, of all places. Have you ever heard Kate mention Abingdon?'

'No, I haven't,' said Cousin. 'But, come to think of it, she's never actually told us she goes to Reading, has she? We've just assumed it. We really must get all this straight with her when she comes in.'

But Kate didn't come in, neither that afternoon, nor the next morning, nor the morning after that. By then Tony Knight was seriously concerned and Cousin volunteered to go around to the house where Kate lodged in Kidlington. Here he found that Kate's landlady was equally worried.

'I haven't known what to do for the best. I was thinking of phoning the agency.' Mrs Carter wiped her hands on her apron. 'The last thing she said to me was, "See you Monday", and now it's Wednesday.' She had asked Cousin into the house once he had explained who he was, and they were having a cup of tea in the kitchen. 'And I've not heard a word from her. I must admit I took the liberty of looking in her room. I knew she wouldn't mind. All her clothes and things are there. She meant to come back, I'm sure.'

'Yes, I'm sure she did, too.'

Cousin gave Mrs Carter a sympathetic smile. He was an observant character, and he had noticed that, though the house, like its owner, was scrupulously clean and tidy, there were clear signs of poverty. The bit of carpet in the hall was badly worn, and Mrs Carter's cardigan had a neat darn at the elbow.

'Mrs Carter, I hate to ask you this,' he said, 'but what about rent? Did Miss Minden owe you anything?'

Mrs Carter shook her grey head. 'That she didn't. She paid me every Friday, a week in advance, and I never once had to remind her. It's not the rent that's worrying me, Mr Cousin,' she added truthfully. 'I liked Miss Minden, and I'm terribly afraid something might have happened to her. You hear of such dreadful stories these days—'

'Yes, I suppose you do, but—You haven't a phone number for her, have you, Mrs Carter, or the address of a relation or anything like that? Somewhere we might try to contact her.'

'Only Mr Knight's.'

For the third or fourth time Mrs Carter wiped her hands on her apron. The nervous gesture had begun to irritate Cousin. Besides, it was clear that Mrs Carter had no idea where Kate might be. He thanked her for the tea, promised to keep in touch and said goodbye.

Knight had fared no better with his own inquiries. He had telephoned Kate's former employers, who had pointed out that it was well over a year since she had worked for them, and had suggested the police. As a last resort Knight had tried the phone number left by the woman who had wanted to speak to Mrs Minden, but as soon as he mentioned the purpose of his call she had again immediately cut the connection.

'It'll have to be the police, Peter,' Knight said finally. 'We've got to report Kate as missing. We can't just do nothing and pretend she never was.'

'She won't bless us if she's flown off to Paris with her boyfriend,' Cousin warned. 'Neither will the police if we waste their time.'

'We can't help that. It's not like Kate to go away without telling anyone,' Knight protested. 'She's a considerate girl.'

A considerate girl. It would have made a fitting epitaph for Kate Minden.

CHAPTER 2

Detective Chief Inspector Dick Tansey of the Thames Valley Police Serious Crime Squad was not in the best of tempers.

'The wretched girl has probably gone off somewhere with

her boyfriend,' he said, unknowingly echoing Peter Cousin.

'Alternatively, sir, she's been assaulted and raped, and is lying dead in a ditch somewhere.'

Tansey regarded Detective-Sergeant Hilary Greenway with cold grey eyes. It was mainly her presence that accounted for his irritability. He didn't like working with women. Sergeant Greenway was no exception. The fact that she was not only efficient, but also physically attractive, with her dark hair and wide green eyes, made no difference; if anything, it made matters worse. He distrusted her cool, laid-back manner, which sometimes seemed to him to border on insolence, though so far he had never known her overstep what might be called 'the mark'. Her last comment had been typical; one could take it how one pleased.

'At least that would make it an interesting case,' he replied, and waited.

But Sergeant Greenway merely said, 'Yes, sir.'

The other reason for his dissatisfaction, Tansey was prepared to admit, was the fact that he had been lumbered with this new case. Strictly speaking, missing persons hardly came into the category of serious crime, especially if they had merely been missing for a few days. Often no crime at all, serious or otherwise, was involved. Someone or other had merely taken it into his or her head to walk out suddenly —on husband, or wife, or lover, or a commitment of some kind.

Nevertheless, as always Headquarters was short of staff because of leave and sickness and, as Tansey had just successfully completed a murder inquiry, he had been the officer most vulnerable to the plea that it surely couldn't take much time or effort to look into Kate Minden's disappearance.

He pushed back his chair, and stood up. 'Okay, let's go,' he said. 'Maybe, if we're lucky, we'll get the whole damned thing wrapped up today.'

Dick Tansey strode out of the room, leaving his sergeant

to follow. He was tall and lean, in his middle thirties. Efficient and ambitious, he had done well in the Force, but to the detriment of his private life. His wife had left him some five years ago, taking their baby daughter with her, and he had subsequently given her the divorce she had sought. At the time he had been too busy to miss them, and by now he seldom regretted the loss of either his wife or his daughter. He didn't think of himself as a lonely man, and he would have been surprised to learn that Hilary Greenway —who was aware of his history—was rather sorry for him.

Hurrying to keep up with the Chief Inspector, Sergeant Greenway reached Tansey's unmarked police car in time to open the door for her senior officer. Then she slid neatly behind the wheel and started the engine.

'To the estate agency, sir?'

Tansey nodded. The question was unnecessary. It was A. J. Knight who had first reported Kate Minden missing, so obviously inquiries must commence with him, especially as his office was only minutes away.

They found both Knight and Cousin waiting for them anxiously. 'We'd better go into our private office,' Knight said, 'but we'll leave the door open so that we can see if anyone comes in.'

Tansey nodded as they fussed around with chairs. Then Knight explained the circumstances that had persuaded them to call the police and, with Cousin's help, recounted what they knew about Kate. It was surprisingly little.

'Mr Cousin, you say you dropped Miss Minden outside the main entrance to the Randolph Hotel in Beaumont Street around five o'clock last Friday,' Tansey said. 'You've done this before?'

'Oh yes. It was always what she wanted. She said it gave her a chance to do a spot of shopping before going along to Gloucester Green to catch her bus for Reading.'

'You're sure it was the Reading bus she caught? You've seen her get on it?'

'Why, no, never,' Cousin said slowly. 'But—'

'All right.' Tansey interrupted him. 'Last Friday, would anyone else have seen you drop Miss Minden?' He paused and added quickly, as Cousin looked surprised, 'Someone who might have noticed which way she went?'

'Perhaps. There were a lot of people around, but I didn't pay any particular attention to them.'

'What time did you meet these clients of yours in Cowley, Mr Cousin?'

'I didn't. I waited until after six, but they never showed. I phoned them the next day. There seemed to be some muddle about the appointment. Or perhaps they weren't really keen.' Cousin shrugged. 'That sort of thing's not unusual in this business. People are funny; sometimes they find it embarrassing to tell you a place won't do. Anyway, what's this got to do with Kate?' He had begun to sound slightly exasperated.

Tansey didn't answer. Nor did he pursue the point. He asked if a photograph of the missing girl was available and Knight, riffling through a drawer, found several. They had all been taken by Cousin in the firm's offices, and had been intended for publicity purposes.

'Here you are,' he said, passing the prints to the Chief Inspector. 'You can see she was a real beauty with that lovely red hair. Incidentally, I forgot to mention that a lady phoned on Friday. She left an Abingdon number and seemed eager that Kate should get in touch with her at once, but she was a bit odd. She certainly wasn't a client. For one thing, she rang off the moment I asked for her name.'

Knight explained further, and produced the slip of paper on which he had noted the number. Hilary Greenway took it from him. She went outside and, through the open door of the office and the display windows, they could see her using the phone in the police car.

'Thanks,' Tansey said. 'We should be able to trace the

caller, and it could be useful. Anything else you remember,
let me know—or, of course, if you hear from Miss Minden.'

With a casual nod the Chief Inspector left the two men,
neither of whom seemed especially reassured by his visit. He
joined Hilary Greenway in the car, but made no comment on
the interview. 'We'll try the landlady now,' he said.

Their carphone buzzed as they drew up in front of the
house where Kate Minden had lodged. Tansey seized the
receiver, listened and made a quick note. He was smiling
with satisfaction as the conversation ended.

'They're getting quite efficient at Headquarters,' he remarked. 'That took no time at all. M. R. Sherry of Mimosa
Cottage, High Lane, Abingdon. Her call could be irrelevant,
but I suppose we'd better look into it.' Tansey opened the
car door. 'But first let's see what this Mrs Carter has to say
about our Miss or Mrs Minden, Sergeant.'

In fact, Kate's landlady had nothing to add to what
she had already told Peter Cousin. But, almost constantly
wiping her hands on her apron in an excess of nervousness,
she took them up the steep, narrow staircase to Kate's
bedsitter. She explained that Miss Minden made her own
breakfast and took sandwiches for lunch and that her rent
included a hot supper, which Mrs Carter cooked for her
from Mondays to Thursdays.

'She was a splendid lodger. Never no trouble,' Mrs Carter
said. 'I do hope nothing's happened to her.'

'Yes, indeed,' Tansey said meaninglessly.

He was looking around the bedsitting-room, which was
neat and clean, but completely impersonal. There were no
photographs, no *objets d'art*, not even a plant or a poster,
only a couple of books—and these belonged to the local
public library. Outside of a hotel he had rarely seen a room
that looked less interesting, but its appearance confirmed
what he had already begun to suspect—that Kate Minden
was a strange girl with some secret she was determined to

hide. Against his will the Chief Inspector was becoming intrigued.

He watched as Hilary Greenway opened and shut the drawers of a small chest, and searched through the clothes in a cupboard. She gave no sign that she was doing anything other than going through a formality, but Tansey knew she could be trusted to make acute observations. He waited until she had finished before trying to offer Mrs Carter some reassurance, which he thought was probably false. He promised to be in touch.

'Well?' he asked as they drew away from the kerb.

'No letters, no cheque-book, nothing personal at all, sir. From her clothes I'd say she's a careful shopper. She'd got a good winter coat, for instance, and a nice pair of boots, but there's a minimum of everything, including cosmetics, and no jewellery at all. Somehow it doesn't fit with the picture of her that Knight and Cousin drew—an attractive young woman who spends every weekend with a boyfriend.'

'She could be saving up to get married,' Tansey suggested.

Greenway shook her head. 'Somehow I doubt it, sir. But she's certainly no spendthrift. Even those lodgings are— pathetic. She's made absolutely no effort over her room. Surely she could have afforded to spend a little to cheer it up.'

'Maybe,' said Tansey. He thought of his own house, hardly a home since his wife had left him. He knew that Sergeant Hilary Greenway lived by herself in digs, and he found himself wondering about the details of her way of life.

By now they had reached Beaumont Street in Oxford, and turned in through the archway to the Randolph Hotel's parking area. Eventually they found the porter who had been on duty the previous Friday, but he had been busy with new arrivals. Shown a photograph of Kate Minden, he gave a low whistle and said, busy or not, he'd have remembered her if he'd seen her.

At the bus station, the driver of a bus which had just arrived from Reading introduced himself as Malcolm, and claimed he certainly hadn't driven the girl in the photograph to Reading or anywhere else on that Friday or any time when he'd been on duty. 'But she's a stunner,' he added almost casually. 'There's not many girls around with red hair like that.'

'You sound as if you've seen her,' Hilary Greenway said quickly.

'Yes, I think I did, several weekends ago. She was running as if she was late, and I only caught a glimpse before she flung herself on to a coach that had begun to shut its doors. That's if it was her, but if it wasn't it was someone very like her. And, as I said, there's not many like that.'

'I suppose you didn't notice what coach this girl caught, did you?' Tansey inquired tentatively.

'Why, sure. It was Charlie's. The Abingdon bus. Hi, Charlie!'

He waved to a short man with broad shoulders, who was chatting to a colleague. Charlie dropped his cigarette butt on the ground, extinguished it with a heel and came over to them. The first coach driver introduced them and Tansey showed Charlie his photograph of Kate.

''Course I know her,' Charlie said. 'She rides with me regular-like. There on Friday and back on Monday, except when it's a holiday, and then it's back on Tuesday.'

Tansey couldn't believe his luck. 'Last Friday as usual?'

'No. I was surprised. You see, as a rule I pick her up at the stop down by Christ Church, though she sometimes comes here to the bus station. Anyways, she was neither place on Friday, and I wondered if she might be sick.' He stared at the detectives doubtfully. 'Has something happened to her, then?'

'We hope not,' Greenway said, and before the driver could speak again, asked the crucial question. 'And where do you drop her?'

'Drop her? Why, at the High Lane stop, on the edge of Abingdon. That's where I pick her up, too. But she wasn't there Monday, if that's what you're going to ask.'

It wasn't the question he had immediately in mind, but Tansey didn't say so. Instead, 'Was anyone at all waiting for you at the Christ Church stop on Friday?'

'Only an elderly woman with a suitcase. I've no idea who she was,' said Charlie. He glanced at his watch. 'Gawd! I'm late. I'll have the inspector on me if I don't get going.'

He hurried off, leaving the Chief Inspector to thank Malcolm, who had just come off duty and would have been happy to continue the conversation. But there was nothing more to be learnt at the coach station. Clearly Abingdon, not Reading, was the place to which Kate Minden had gone so religiously each weekend.

'Sir,' said Sergeant Greenway, when they had cleared the Oxford traffic and were on their way to Abingdon. 'Your question about people waiting at the Christ Church stop? Were you thinking some man might have picked Kate Minden up there?'

'Why not? Attractive girl. Pleasant young man "going her way". I was hoping someone might have seen it.'

'She wasn't a fool!' exclaimed Greenway. 'She was twenty-seven, and an experienced secretary! She wouldn't have fallen for that old line.'

There was a long moment of silence after this outburst, while Hilary Greenway wished she had spoken less vehemently and prepared herself to accept whatever acid rebuke the Chief Inspector might produce. She was surprised when he said quite gently:

'Anyone can be deceived. It might have been someone she knew—even slightly. Someone she believed she could trust.'

'I hadn't thought of that, sir,' Greenway admitted. 'And I suppose Peter Cousin might not have dropped her off at

the Randolph. She'd have agreed if *he*'d offered her a lift to
Abingdon.'

'Possibly.' Tansey had taken a map of the district from a
pocket in the door of the car. 'Do you know where High
Lane is, Sergeant?'

It was only three months since Hilary Greenway had
been promoted to sergeant and transferred to the Kidlington
Serious Crime Squad; before that she had been stationed in
Maidenhead. But she had spent a great deal of her recent
spare time studying maps and walking and driving around
in her old Mini, in order to familiarize herself with the
geography of Oxford and its immediate surroundings. She
was determined to make a success of her new rank and job.

'I think I can find it, sir,' she said, hoping she was right.

Indeed, she nearly missed the turning, and had to brake
sharply, which annoyed her. But the Chief Inspector, who
had been jerked forward against his seat-belt, made no
comment.

High Lane was, in fact, a residential street with houses
on either side, and Mimosa Cottage turned out to be the
third house on the left. Like its fellows, it was a bungalow
with an attached garage and a reasonable amount of land.
It was not new, all the homes apparently having been put
up by a speculative builder in the 'fifties but, again like its
neighbours, it was well cared for, and the front garden was
immaculate.

'Respectable, retired, middle-class, with a pension and a
little over, but not too much,' Tansey murmured as he shut
the gate behind him.

He had let Greenway go first, because there was a child
sitting on the step in front of the half-open front door.
The day was reasonably mild, but it was the beginning of
October and the child—she was a girl—was warmly dressed
in corduroy trousers and a thick sweater. She stood up,
holding the large rag doll she had been nursing, and turned
solemn eyes on the two officers as they came up the path.

She was about five years old, and she reminded Tansey that his own daughter would be that age now—though she would never have inherited the glorious red hair that this child possessed.

Hilary Greenway crouched down, so that her face was level with that of the little girl. 'Hello,' she said. 'We've come to see your Mummy. Is she in?'

The child shook her head. Then, dropping the doll, she turned and fled into the house. 'Gran!' she called. 'Gran!'

An elderly woman came to the door. Her hair was white and her skin was lined, but it was clear that she had once been beautiful. She stared at Tansey and Greenway aggressively.

'Yes? What do you want?'

Tansey held out his warrant card. 'Detective Chief Inspector Tansey.' He introduced himself. 'And Detective Sergeant Greenway. You're Mrs Sherry?'

'I'm Martha Sherry.' She had been pale before the question, but now all the remaining colour had fled from her face, and her eyes had become dark with fear. 'It's—is it about Katerina?' She had difficulty enunciating the question.

'If that's Kate Minden, yes, Mrs Sherry, it is about her. May we come in? There are a few questions we'd like you to answer, if you would.' Tansey spoke gently.

Without a reply Mrs Sherry led the way into the front room, which was full of books and flowers and photographs —a happy, lived-in room, with one or two good pieces of furniture. The child had rejoined them, but disappeared obediently when told to go and play in the back garden.

'That is my granddaughter,' Mrs Sherry explained unnecessarily. Having started to speak, she seemed to feel compelled to continue. 'Her name's Zelda. She's Katerina's child. When her—her father—died, and Katerina moved to Kidlington, she came to live with me—I'm a widow; my husband passed away years ago. It's a good arrangement, not perfect, perhaps, but—' She stopped abruptly, as if suddenly aware that the flood of words was out of character.

There was a pause, but she raised a hand and went on before Tansey could ask his first question. 'I know. I know. Katerina's disappeared, hasn't she? Until last Friday she's never missed a weekend with us—with Zelda and me—and I don't know what to think. That's what you've come about, isn't it? Well, I've heard nothing at all from her, and I've been so troubled. Do you know where she is?'

'No, Mrs Sherry. I wish we did. All we can tell you is that she's not had an accident; all the hospitals have been checked. And we know she left her office on Friday as usual. A man called Peter Cousin, who works at Knight's Estate Agency, gave her a lift as far as Beaumont Street in Oxford, but she doesn't seem to have been seen since.'

'Katerina's mentioned Peter Cousin,' Mrs Sherry said unexpectedly. 'Once or twice she got the impression he wanted to ask her to go out with him, but she didn't want to, and she tried to discourage him.'

'Does she have a regular boyfriend?' Greenway asked.

'No. She didn't want anyone, not after—' Quickly Mrs Sherry corrected what she had been about to say. 'Katerina works hard during the week, and at weekends she devotes herself to Zelda.'

'And you've no idea where she might have gone? Or can you think of anyone who might know?'

There was a fractional hesitation before Mrs Sherry shook her head. 'No. I've been thinking about it since Friday and, apart from the agency and that Mrs Carter where Katerina lives in Kidlington, I don't know of anyone to ask.'

'Why not the police, Mrs Sherry? Why didn't you report the matter here in Abingdon, instead of phoning your daughter's office anonymously, and leaving it to them?'

'Me? Me?' Mrs Sherry was obviously worried by the question. 'I don't know. I hoped she'd turn up. I didn't want to say the wrong thing to the agency. I don't know.'

'I see,' said Tansey slowly, considering whether or not to take matters further at this stage. He decided to change the subject.

'Your daughter keeps a room here, I imagine?' he said.

'Yes. It's next to Zelda's.'

'Could we see it, please?'

Mrs Sherry led them along a passageway and opened the door to a small but cheerful bedroom, very different from the bedsitter in Kidlington. Here were photographs and prints on the walls, books on shelves, pleasant curtains and matching bedspread—a room on which effort had been expended. Quite clearly, this was Kate Minden's real home.

Hilary Greenway looked inquiringly at Mrs Sherry and received a nod before opening drawers and cupboards. There were not many clothes, but once again they were carefully chosen, and of good quality.

It was obvious that no more was to be learnt in High Lane, and that Mrs Sherry would be of no further immediate help, so, soon afterwards, the detectives took their leave, promising to keep in touch. By now they both accepted that if Kate Minden—Mrs Katerina Minden—was to be found, alive or dead, a lot more work would need to be done, a lot of research undertaken, and a lot of doorbells rung and questions asked.

CHAPTER 3

The second girl disappeared on the following Saturday. Mary Rust was her name, and in background and character she could scarcely have been more different from Kate Minden.

Mary was seventeen—and, considering the state of current mores, a surprisingly sheltered and unsophisticated seventeen. She had, for instance, never spent a night away from home. She was an only child, and she lived with her parents over the health food store which her father owned and managed in the market town of Colombury in the Cotswolds. She had attended the local school and, after failing to distinguish herself in any way, had left at the earliest legal moment and had started work in the shop. The business brought the Rust family a moderate living, and Mrs Rust, who was a semi-invalid, didn't work outside their home, except for an occasional turn behind the counter in the shop.

The Rusts were eccentric; many people thought them just plain cranks. They belonged to a religious sect which no one had ever heard of, but which heavily stressed prohibition rather than enjoyment. They were strict vegetarians, and never touched alcohol. They disapproved of dancing, music and almost every form of entertainment, and they did not possess a television set. Mrs Rust was a fair needlewoman, and made clothes for herself and Mary, and even some for her husband. Apart from minding the store, Mr Rust did all the cooking, about which he was very particular. From her earliest years Mary had been trained to help with the housework.

For recreation they read good books, selected by Mr Rust from the public library, and went for walks to commune with nature. But what with one thing and another, and one chore and another, there was scant time for such pleasures. Once a year the store was closed and they spent two weeks with Mr Rust's unmarried sister in Sussex, where the scenery was different but the routine similar. Miss Rust was of the same persuasion as her brother.

The family went neither to church nor to chapel, took no part in any civic or charitable affairs and, needless to say, had no friends. It was a strange, lonely life for Mary, which altered little as she got older.

It was ironic that, by some odd quirk of genetics, the Rusts, who were an ordinary-looking couple, should have produced a beautiful daughter. Mary had long brown hair, an oval face and large blue eyes which instantly attracted attention. But she was a shy girl. She found it hard to mix with her contemporaries, and sometimes even to understand their slang. And as she had never been allowed to accept any invitations or take part in any out-of-school activities, she had soon been left alone by all her would-be friends, but two.

One took the form of a large plain girl called Betty Dawson. She and Mary had gone through school together, class by class. They liked the same subjects and the same teachers, and giggled at the same simple jokes. And when they left at sixteen they had identical negligible qualifications. Betty became an assistant at a local dress shop managed by one of her aunts, just as Mary joined the family store. They continued to be friends.

The Rusts tended to approve of Betty Dawson, in spite of the fact that her mother was a divorcée; to be more accurate, they didn't actively disapprove of the daughter. Her mother, who held a responsible position at the local public library, had in her favour that she was a regular consumer of health foods, and Betty herself had an air of childish innocence which was completely belied by the truth.

The Rusts would have been horrified to learn that the innocent walks with Betty which they sanctioned often led to the local cinema, and that Mary had learnt more about sex from Betty—at least in theory—than she ever had from the lessons at school. They would have been even more horrified had they known that Betty's current boyfriend sometimes accompanied them on their expeditions, and brought his cousin.

The cousin in question—one Brian Quayle—was the other exception—and an exception of whom Mr and Mrs Rust were quite unaware. If the Rusts accepted Betty Dawson as a suitable companion for their daughter, nothing would have made them accept Brian Quayle. Brian had been seen drinking beer outside the Windrush Arms last summer. Brian had been stopped by the police for driving his employer's van at excessive speed. Above all, Brian worked as a butcher's assistant; any weekday you could see him cutting up lamb chops or heaving great carcases of meat around. Mr Rust had once told him to stop coming into the health food store because he smelt of blood.

Nevertheless, Brian was not deterred by this snub. He had been in love with Mary Rust, or so he believed, since the age of eight. Now he was nineteen, six feet tall, big-boned, red-faced, with large square hands and a gentle manner. He was not exactly Mary's idea of a Prince Charming, but she was flattered by his persistence, and she found it exciting to hold hands in the darkness of the cinema, to feel his cheek rub softly against hers and sometimes to let him stroke her breast through her thin blouse. In her ignorance Mary failed to realize how few boys would have been content for so long with such limited favours; and if the truth were told even Brian was becoming impatient.

In fact, Mr Rust's accusation that he smelt of blood was quite untrue. Brian was careful with his appearance, not least if he was expecting to meet Mary. And on the Saturday that Mary disappeared he had taken special care because he hoped that it would be a day to remember. In spite of her parents' attitudes, he had made up his mind to suggest to Mary that they become secretly engaged, and if she accepted . . .

As he pulled on his new green slacks over his clean underpants he felt himself hardening in anticipation, and he grinned broadly.

The weather had remained warm for the time of year, and on that Saturday the sky was a pale, misty blue, the sun bright. Leaves, red, brown, yellow, fluttered down from the trees, but there was no sign of the melancholy usually associated with autumn. Betty Dawson called for Mary Rust

promptly at two o'clock; the hours of Mary's one free
afternoon each week were not to be wasted.

Betty's round face was at its most innocent, but Mary
could sense her friend's excitement, and it communicated
itself to her. Questioned, however, Betty merely squeezed
Mary's arm and told her to wait and see.

Colombury was a small town, not much more than an
overgrown village, busy on market days and popular with
tourists to the Cotswolds, but fortunately still spared much
semi-urban sprawl on its outskirts. Those who knew the
district, as Mary and Betty did, could cut through fields
and reach narrow, leafy lanes in no time. But it was a long
walk to Copley Wood, and Mary was surprised when Betty
finally named this as their destination.

'At least, that's where *you're* going, Mary dear,' Betty
corrected herself. 'And, what's more, you're going to enjoy
yourself.'

Copley Wood had something of a reputation as a meeting-
place for lovers, and Mary said, 'Are the boys coming? And
what about you?' She was puzzled and slightly anxious.

'Just you and Brian.' Betty giggled. 'Here he is, waiting
for you.'

They had come through a field gate into a lane, and there
was Brian, sitting astride a powerful-looking motorbike, a
red helmet on his head and a white one dangling from his
large, square hand. He dismounted when he saw the girls,
and gave them each a brotherly kiss on the cheek. For the
moment Mary was more interested in the motorbike than
in Brian.

'Is that yours, then?' she asked at once.

'What? Me own a big Honda? How could I afford it? You
must be joking, luv. A chap I know at the garage lent it to
me.' He grinned at her. 'Care for a spin?'

'I've never been on one of them before,' Mary said doubtfully.

Betty and Brian exchanged glances. 'You'll love it,' Betty

said firmly. She helped Mary on with her helmet, seated her on the pillion and showed her how to put her arms around Brian's waist to hold on to him ''Bye,' she called, as Brian accelerated down the lane. 'Have fun!'

After some initial apprehension Mary found that she *was* having fun. Clutching Brian tightly, she experienced a wonderful sense of exhilaration, partly due to the closeness of the youth's body and partly to the wind rushing past as her long brown hair streamed out behind them. They reached Copley Wood too soon for her liking, but she reminded herself that the ride back to Colombury was yet to come.

Brian pushed the motorbike along a narrow path, and forced his way between two bushes into a small clearing. Mary followed without question. He propped the bike against a tree, and opened one of the containers beside the back wheel. He had brought a thin blanket, which he spread on the ground, some cans of beer for himself and an orange drink for Mary.

'Another time we could bring sandwiches, and have a proper picnic,' he said.

'That would be nice,' Mary agreed, 'but it's not usually warm enough for that in October.' She gave a small shiver. 'It's okay walking, but it's a bit chilly in here under the trees.'

Many girls other than Mary Rust would have intended the last remark as an invitation. Brian knew that it wasn't, but he pulled Mary down on to the blanket and put one leg over her. He kissed her gently.

'I'll keep you warm,' he said. 'I'll keep you warm for always if you'll let me. Mary, I've been thinking. I know we can't get married for a while yet, but if you agreed we could get engaged, secret-like. I'm not good enough for you, of course. You're so beautiful. But I do love you, and I mean to get on, open my own shop, have a whole chain perhaps.'

He went on talking, murmuring endearments as he drew a picture of a fantastic future, in which at that moment he himself half-believed. At the same time he was stroking her, kissing her and eventually unbuttoning her blouse. Mary lay, happy, contented and excited by his words and his caresses, which had never before been so bold. She opened her mouth to let him give her what he called a French kiss, and shifted her body so as to accommodate his weight more comfortably. It was not until he pulled her skirt up to her thighs and slid his hands under her pants that she pushed him away.

'No, Brian! No!' she cried suddenly. 'There's someone watching us!'

Mary struggled to sit up, pulling down her skirt with one hand and pointing over Brian's shoulder with the other. Cursing under his breath, he rolled off her and looked in the direction she was pointing. He could see nothing.

'There's no one there, luv. Come on, Mary. I want you, luv.' He pushed her down and started nuzzling her hair. 'Don't you want me?' he murmured.

'I—I don't know, Brian.' Mary's mood had changed. She was no longer happy and aroused, but nervous and afraid. She wanted to leave this place. 'Anyway, not here. I'm sure somebody was watching. I saw the bush move.'

'Rubbish! Don't be silly, Mary. Come on, luv.'

He forced her down and unzipped his slacks. He was breathing heavily. He couldn't stop now. He wanted her too badly. She was his, and he was going to screw her.

By 5.30 that afternoon Mrs Rust was wondering where Mary could have got to, and Mr Rust was standing by the window, hoping to see her come running down the street. So far neither of them had voiced their anxiety. But by 6.00 it was getting dark, and Mary had still not returned.

'Where can she be?' Mrs Rust said at last. 'It's not like her to be late. Do you think she could have had an accident or something?'

'Betty would have let us know.'

'Mary might have twisted her ankle, say, and Betty might be helping her walk home.'

Mr Rust grunted. His wife's tentatively offered explanation was possible, but not probable, he thought. Still, he loved his daughter and he trusted her. She was a good girl, but when Mary went out with Betty Dawson for an afternoon walk, she was always back long before this, so that he couldn't help but be anxious. He wasn't a fool and he knew that the world was full of temptations and was quite aware of the kinds of licence other girls were allowed.

'I shall go and telephone the Dawsons,' he said half an hour later. 'Betty's mother should be home by now and I'll speak to her.'

The Rusts had no private telephone, but there was one in the health food store below. Mr Rust went downstairs. It was absurd, he told himself, but he found he was reluctant to call Mrs Dawson and admit that his daughter had stayed out late and he had no idea where she was.

Betty answered the Dawson's phone herself. She said hello with enthusiasm, and was taken aback when Mr Rust announced his identity. Though, according to her teachers, Betty was far from clever, she was nevertheless quick-witted, and she had a great sense of self-preservation. She lied easily.

'Mary and I had a long walk,' she said, 'out towards Copley Wood. I was tired when we got back, and I left Mary at the bottom of Farley's Lane. You mean she's not home yet, Mr Rust?'

'I wouldn't be ringing you about her if she was, would I?' Rust said roughly.

'Well, I'm sorry, but I can't help you. I expect she went to visit a friend and forgot the time. Excuse me, Mr Rust.' For a moment she covered her receiver with her hand. Then she said, 'I must go, Mr Rust. My mum's calling me. Goodbye.'

As soon as she had hung up, Betty Dawson stood by her phone, thinking. Then, knowing that her mother was safely occupied elsewhere in the house, she dialled Brian Quayle's number. She was careful what she said, but she made sure that she would see him at the disco later that night.

For his part, Mr Rust was furious at Betty's abrupt ending of their conversation. This was the last time that Mary was going out with that Dawson girl, he vowed, as he returned upstairs to his wife. Their simple evening meal was ready, and they sat down to it though neither of them could eat.

'Something's happened to her,' said Mrs Rust eventually, and she began to cry quietly. 'She'd be home by now otherwise. It's gone half seven.'

'I'm going round to the Dawsons,' said Mr Rust. It was the only positive action he could think of. 'I'm not sure that Betty doesn't know more than she said. Maybe face to face she'll be a mite more communicative.'

But Betty Dawson was not at home. Her mother opened the door. She was polite, but not especially friendly. Mr Rust thought he heard a man cough in the front room, and wondered who she was entertaining, though it was none of his business. She didn't ask him in, and he had to explain his business on the doorstep.

It was a waste of effort. Mrs Dawson knew nothing about Mary. Betty had gone to the disco with her boyfriend. She supposed Mary could be with them. When Mr Rust protested that this was most unlikely, she merely suggested the police and said good night.

Reluctantly, and with a heavy heart, Mr Rust took Mrs Dawson's advice. He went immediately to the local police station to tell Sergeant Court, the officer who had for many years been in charge there, that his daughter, Mary, was missing.

This rapid reporting, and some quick thinking on the part of Sergeant Court and the inspector on duty at the Kidlington headquarters, led to the ruination of what was left of the weekend for Detective Chief Inspector Tansey and Detective-Sergeant Greenway.

CHAPTER 4

As the good people of Colombury went their various ways that following Sunday morning—some to church, some to chapel, and some to remain lounging at home till the pubs opened—the news of Mary Rust's disappearance spread throughout the town. It positively buzzed with rumour and excitement.

The excitement intensified when Sergeant Court was spotted showing two strangers, instantly identified as plain-clothes detectives from the Thames Valley Force, into their car, and the car was subsequently seen parked outside the Rusts' health food store. It did not remain there long. Neither Mr Rust nor his wife was very helpful.

'I've told you all I know,' Mr Rust said at last with suppressed irritation. 'And it's the same as what I told Sergeant Court last night. Our Mary went for a walk with this girl, Betty Dawson, and she hasn't come home since. We don't know where she is and we're worried sick.'

'You say she was a happy, contented girl,' Detective Chief Inspector Tansey said. 'Did she have lots of friends?'

'A boyfriend?' suggested Detective-Sergeant Greenway.

'No she did *not*. She was a good girl. She wasn't like other young people. These days most of them'll break every commandment in the Good Book and commit sins I wouldn't even mention in front of Mrs Rust. Nor in your hearing, miss.' The last remark was addressed to Sergeant Greenway, who for a moment was slightly nonplussed at this unaccustomed gallantry.

Tansey, who had been warned by Sergeant Court of Mary's strict upbringing, said mildly, 'Mary was seventeen, Mr Rust. She wasn't a child. Girls get married at that age.'

This comment produced an unexpected tirade from Mr

Rust—so vehement that his wife had to intervene. Tansey was shaken. It was a long time since his personal morals, or his integrity as a police officer, had been attacked by anyone, let alone by a respectable, apparently law-abiding citizen. But he made no effort to defend himself. He ignored Rust's words.

Instead he addressed himself to the woman, saying coldly, 'Mrs Rust, we should like to inspect your daughter's room. Will you show us the way?'

'Why?' Mr Rust demanded before his wife could reply.

Greenway said quietly, 'It's usual police procedure, Mr Rust. You've reported your daughter as missing, and her room might provide some clue as to the reason for her disappearance.'

Mr Rust turned his gaze on her. 'Then you go, miss. I'm not having some strange man touching my girl's underwear and things with his filthy hands.'

Tansey restrained himself. 'I'll wait for you in the car, Sergeant,' he intervened as he saw Hilary Greenway draw a sharp breath; he guessed it was about to emerge as a comment better left unsaid.

'If you wish, sir,' she said, swallowing her intended words, and giving the 'sir' its full quota of respect, 'I'll be as quick as I can.'

She was as good as her word. Within ten minutes she was sliding into the car alongside the Chief Inspector. 'Nothing, sir,' she said. 'I made a pretty thorough search of the usual places a girl might hide letters or photographs—under the mattress, in the drawer behind her undies and so on. There was a box on top of the wardrobe, but it only contained old Christmas cards. Otherwise the room was as innocent as that revolting father of hers would have wished.'

Tansey grinned. 'I see,' he said. 'Well, I suppose that means that Rust didn't lie to us, like that Mrs Sherry. Remember all that nonsense about Katerina being a widow. I wish we'd taken time to run everyone through records before we called on her. Then we'd have known—as she must have known—that husband Steve was far from being dead, and had been doing a stint inside for robbery with violence. What we're not sure she knew is that Steve Minden had been released a couple of weeks ago, and, what's more, had missed a call on his probation officer. If he doesn't show up soon, there'll be a warrant out for him. Anyway, that Sherry woman annoyed me. She must have been quite aware she couldn't pull the wool over our eyes for long.'

'I'm not sure you can blame her for much, sir, except being stupid,' said Greenway as she started the engine. 'She's not young, and she's probably been telling her story for so long she half-believes it's true.'

'Maybe,' Tansey admitted. 'Anyway, the important thing is what line she takes if Minden doesn't show up, and we have to put out a call for him. She could know where he might be.'

'I should think in that case she'd be only too pleased to come clean. She could well be afraid what the husband might do—might have done—to Kate and might try to do with the child. And that's another point,' Greenway added thoughtfully, 'if she'd known that Minden was free and on the loose would she have let little Zelda play so openly in front of the house?'

'Maybe,' Tansey said again. 'Maybe she would and maybe she wouldn't. But it's a good point.' Then he changed the subject. 'The other oddity is their financial situation,' he went on. 'Okay, we now know that Mrs Sherry's money is locked up in a pension and an annuity and will die with her. But we also know that Mimosa Cottage is free of mortgage, and so should be worth a quid or two. Why is Kate Minden so keen to skimp and save? For the kid's sake, do you think? Does she expect to send the child to school at Benenden later on?'

'Scarcely Benenden, sir, but perhaps somewhere a bit better than the local comprehensive. Poor Kate!' Hilary

Greenway spoke with real sympathy. 'I suspect she wanted to make up to little Zelda for her father's shortcomings.'

Dick Tansey grunted. He had had loving parents, but there had been no money to spare. He had been a clever boy, and had made his own way on scholarships. When his father died he had helped his mother. He had inherited nothing from either of them. Nor had he expected to, and he saw no reason why anyone else should have expectations.

'We'd better forget Kate Minden for the moment,' he said, 'and concentrate on young Mary. Let's hope that girlfriend of hers knows something about her that her wretched parents don't.'

Mrs Dawson and Betty, warned by telephone that two detectives would be calling on them, were waiting, each of them with some trepidation. Betty had told her mother the truth—or most of the truth—about the previous afternoon's expedition, and Mrs Dawson had been able to make a good guess about any private arrangements Betty might have made with Brian.

At first she had been amused, rather than censorious, at the part Betty had played in organizing what she supposed could be called an assignation. But, on reflection, she became alarmed for Mary, and had no wish for Betty to get into trouble with the police. However, she was astute enough to insist that her daughter told Tansey and Greenway the whole story, though she suggested that Betty should avoid any speculation as to Brian's intentions in the course of the motorbike ride. After all, it was clearly impossible for Mary to be seen on the back of Brian's bike in or near the town; all Betty had done was arrange a meeting-place for the two of them.

When Betty had finished, and answered some initial questions, Mrs Dawson added firmly, 'You've got to appreciate what Mr and Mrs Rust are like. They're impossible

—quite impossible. They're living in another century. A girl of Mary's age, especially one with her looks—she's exceptionally lovely—should be having a good time, going to discos and parties, enjoying herself, having lots of boy-friends. But not Mary Rust. She wasn't allowed to do anything or go anywhere—not even to the movies. We all felt sorry for her. Chief Inspector, I'm not condoning what Betty did. She shouldn't have deceived the Rusts or lied to Mr Rust afterwards, but I can understand what made her act that way.'

'So can I, Mrs Dawson,' Tansey said, pleased to be dealing with a well-spoken and articulate woman. 'In the circumstances I can't blame Betty either, but on this oc-casion her actions seem to have had unfortunate conse-quences. Mary's disappeared, as you know. And until we find her everyone concerned, including you and Betty, must be worried that she might have come to some harm.'

'Of course, Chief Inspector, we *are* worried for Mary, and Betty'll do anything she can to help. Won't you, Betty?'

'Yes, Mum.' Betty Dawson turned to Tansey. 'But, as I said, I left Mary with Brian Quayle, and she'd have been safe with him. He wouldn't have hurt a hair of her head. He's been soft on her—truly soft—since he was a kid.'

'We'll be seeing him ourselves, of course,' Tansey said, 'but it might help if you told us what he's like—what you think of him yourself, for instance.'

'He's big, red-faced, beefy.' Betty laughed suddenly. 'He's a butcher.' When no one shared her amusement at the joke, she quickly smothered her mirth and appeared to be thinking hard. 'I suppose he's not bad-looking, and he's popular. Girls do go for him. But he's got this fix on Mary. And, yes, he's a terrific dancer, though he's so big.'

Tansey would have ignored this final comment, but Greenway said, 'Was he at the disco last night, Betty?'

'Yes, miss—Sergeant. He arrived late. I saw him come in.'

'Alone?'

'Yes. You don't have to bring a partner. And Brian often comes by himself, or with another guy. There are always spare girls.'

'You must have spoken to him, asked him about Mary?' Sergeant Greenway said quietly.

'Sure. I told him Mr Rust had rung because she hadn't got home yet. He seemed surprised, but he just said something about the Rusts being a lot of fusspots.'

'That was all? You didn't speak to him again, or dance with him?'

'No, miss.' Betty looked uncomfortable. She wriggled in her chair, and avoided meeting Hilary Greenway's eyes.

'Why not? Don't you usually, Betty?'

'Sure! That's what I said. He's a super dancer, but—oh, hell!—he got drunk last night. He'd been drinking before he got to the disco, I guess, and he had more there. At least—'

'They're only meant to serve soft drinks,' Mrs Dawson interrupted, 'but the boys bring in bottles. What can you expect? Most of them have left school and are working. They're not children any more. A beer or two never hurt anyone, anyway, and they can't afford hard liquor. But there are always the few who have too much and cause trouble.'

'Brian didn't cause any trouble,' Betty said. 'He kind of collapsed, and his mates took him out. One of them said later he'd been sick.'

Tansey had been following this exchange with growing interest. Now he asked, 'Did Brian often drink too much?'

Betty shook her head, and her mother said, 'There's nothing wrong with Brian Quayle, Chief Inspector. He's a good steady lad. I suppose as Mary's so pretty she might do better, but she might do a whole lot worse, too. It's my

opinion that if anything happened to her those parents of
hers are to blame.'

From what he had heard and seen so far Dick Tansey was
inclined to agree, but it was not for him to pass judgement—
at least not at this stage. He asked where the Quayles lived,
and Mrs Dawson directed them.

'They'll be sitting down to their midday meal now,' she
warned.

Tansey looked at his watch. 'I'd no idea it was so late.'

'If you're thinking of eating yourselves, the Windrush
Arms is a good place, and it won't be too full on a Sunday.'

'Good idea. And many thanks for all your help,' Tansey
said as they left.

Then, as they were getting into their car, 'A sensible,
practical woman,' he added to Greenway. 'Now, I suggest
we get some lunch first, and confront the Quayles afterwards. He's unlikely to run off. If he'd been going to make
a dash for it, he'd have gone by now. As for young Mary,
we'll keep an open mind. We don't even know if she's been
done away with yet, and we certainly haven't got enough
evidence to start a search of Copley Wood—'

'But, sir—' Sergeant Greenway opened her mouth to
protest, but was interrupted by the Chief Inspector. 'I know
what you're going to say, Sergeant. Speed is of the essence.
But is it? Let's face it. Our Mary may have just got fed up
and gone off to London or somewhere—perhaps intending
to meet up with this Brian later.'

'I think she sounds much too timid to strike a blow for
freedom like that, sir,' replied Greenway. 'Though I suppose
she could have gone to this aunt where the family say they
spend their annual holiday.'

'But why should she do that? It'd be out of the frying-pan
into the fire, as far as I can see. Maybe Quayle can tell us.'

'It's not very likely he'll be able to tell us anything about
Kate Minden though, is it, sir?' Greenway remarked.

'It's damned unlikely, Sergeant. Frankly, I don't believe

there's any connection between Kate and young Mary, but who knows? Anyway, let's forget them for a short while. Mary may still be alive. But if she's dead in Copley Wood or somewhere round there, a short delay in finding her won't matter. Here's the Windrush Arms. I'll stand you a drink.'

This was the first remotely formal meal that Hilary Greenway had shared with the Chief Inspector. At Headquarters they ate in separate messes, officers separated from other ranks in army style, and when forced to eat out during the present case, they had confined themselves to sandwiches and beer in a pub. Sergeant Greenway detested beer, but forced herself to drink it to avoid any appearance of superiority.

'Gin and tonic? Whisky? Sherry?' Tansey asked as they went into the bar together.

'I'd love a gin and tonic,' Greenway said. Then, thinking that she sounded a little too much like a girl out with her date, she added hurriedly, 'Thank you very much, sir.'

The bar was crowded, but they were lucky enough to find seats side by side on a banquette. When Tansey appeared with their drinks, he remarked that he'd had no trouble booking a table in the dining-room upstairs for 1.15. They chatted desultorily about the Windrush Arms and Colombury and the Cotswolds.

Then Tansey said, 'You'll have the other half?'

'Yes, but let me get it, please.'

'Certainly not! I never let my sergeants buy me anything but pints. If I choose to drink gin or whisky, that's my affair. And don't worry. As a single man, I can afford it.'

'But what about your—' Hilary Greenway stopped abruptly. She felt the flush burning her cheeks. For once she lost her *savoir faire*. 'I—I'm sorry,' she stammered. 'I didn't mean—'

Tansey picked up their glasses. 'Luckily for me,' he said coldly, answering her unfinished question, 'my ex-wife's married a rich man, who insisted on adopting my daughter. Neither of them are anything to do with me any longer.'

'But you must have regrets,' Hilary spoke without thinking.

'Sometimes. Not often now.'

By the time Tansey returned with the drinks his sergeant had regained her composure. She thanked him politely, and she didn't apologize. She acted as if their last conversation were forgotten.

But Tansey wasn't going to let her off so lightly. 'Tell me,' he said conversationally as he sat down beside her. 'What made you choose your present career?'

Hilary Greenway hesitated, then realized she had nothing to lose by answering frankly; it was all in the personnel files, in any case. 'I took a political science degree at London University,' she said. 'Then I got married. My husband was in the Navy. He was killed in the Falklands. I was left with a small pension and a fair number of debts. I needed a job, preferably with prospects. I've always been interested in crime and criminology, so the police were an obvious choice. And that, sir, is my life in a nutshell.'

In his turn he said, 'You must have regrets.'

Hilary hesitated again. Then, 'Not many,' she replied truthfully. 'I suspect we'd have been divorced by now if he'd not been killed. He was a gambler and a womanizer, and our marriage was already a failure.'

Tansey suddenly smiled at her. 'That makes us quits,' he said. He looked at the clock over the bar. 'Let's take our drinks upstairs and go and eat.'

Brian had made no secret of the fact that he intended to spend Saturday afternoon with Mary Rust, so, like the Dawsons, the Quayles were expecting a visit from the police. Throughout their meal they had talked of little other than the girl's disappearance. Only Brian, who had an appalling hangover, failed to contribute a share to the conversation, beyond stating flatly where he had dropped her on the outskirts of Colombury after a motorbike ride and a walk in Copley Wood. His family asked no questions.

'Here they come!' Brian's younger brother, Dave, shouted, dropping the lace curtain back in place across the window as Sergeant Greenway drew up in front of the council house where the Quayles lived.

'Okay. Leave everything to me,' ordered Mr Quayle. 'You show them into the front room, Mother, and make them ask for Brian. Our boy's done nothing wrong, and we mustn't suggest he was waiting for them to come for him. The rest of you stay in here and keep quiet.'

The doorbell rang. Mrs Quayle went to answer it. Doreen, Brian's sister, giggled nervously. Brian himself was perspiring heavily. He had hardly touched his Sunday dinner, but he still felt ill. When Mrs Quayle returned to announce that Detective Chief Inspector Tansey and Detective-Sergeant Greenway would like a word or two with him he followed his father miserably into the front room.

Mr Quayle, who was an older version of Brian, though he was a builder and not a butcher, wasted no time on niceties. 'You've come to see my lad about the Rust girl, I dare say,' he said. 'We heard young Mary had got lost when we were at chapel this morning. What I don't understand is what all the fuss is about. As I understand it, she's not been gone twenty-four hours yet. I thought the police didn't bother till then at the earliest—that's if you ever bothered overmuch.'

'You've been misinformed, Mr Quayle,' said the Chief Inspector evenly. 'We bother. In this case we have two reasons for acting promptly. One, Mary Rust seems to have led an extremely sheltered life.'

'Sheltered?' Mr Quayle gave a great belly laugh. 'The poor little bint wasn't allowed to call her soul her own.'

Tansey ignored him. 'The second reason is that another girl disappeared last week. There may be a connection between the two incidents.' Abruptly he turned to Brian.

'Now, perhaps you'd tell us what you and Mary did yester-day afternoon, Mr Quayle, and where you went. We may ask you to come with us in the car, and show us.'

Brian gobbled a bit, but on the whole he told his story well. He had been worried sick after what had happened the previous afternoon. That was why he had drunk so much more than usual and acquired this frightful hangover. He had been awake half the night with it, and with the need to work out what he would say when he was questioned about Mary, which he knew was almost certain in the circum-stances. But now, faced with the situation he had dreaded, he grew more confident as he proceeded with his tale.

'I'll show you where we went, and where I dropped Mary, if you like,' he volunteered. 'And you can ask Don about me returning the motorbike.'

'Okay. I agree with that,' said Quayle senior. 'But if you're going off with the police, son, I'm coming with you. I'm not having them put words in your mouth you never spoke.'

Tansey got to his feet. 'We'll not trouble either of you any more at present,' he said. 'Thanks for your help. We'll be off. It's Sunday for us, too.'

In the car Sergeant Greenway had difficulty in concealing her indignation. 'Sir,' she said at last, 'that boy Brian was lying. I'm positive he was. His story was much too slick.'

Tansey nodded complacently. 'Sure. He was lying all right. Did you see the relief on his face when I said we were off? And Pa was equally pleased when I pointed out it was our Sunday too. It confirmed his low opinion of the police.'

'And that's a good thing, sir? Will it help to find Mary?' There was an edge to Greenway's voice.

'Perhaps.' Tansey turned to look at Hilary. 'Don't worry, Sergeant. More haste, less speed. We're not going to be idle.'

And with that Sergeant Greenway had to be content.

CHAPTER 5

The third girl—one Linda Jackson—disappeared on the following Friday.

Linda was twenty-one. An undergraduate in her last year at St Anne's College, Oxford, she was reading for a degree in politics and economics, hoping eventually to make a career in journalism. She was a clever girl, and a scholar of her college. Apart from the normal State grant, she was also the beneficiary of an award from a charitable trust, which formed an important part of her income. As her parents were not well off and there were three younger brothers to be educated, she would have found it difficult to go up to Oxford without financial help and, without the trust's award, even more difficult to live as comfortably as she did. Conscious of her luck, she worked hard.

But she also played hard, and enjoyed herself. She was an enthusiastic member of the Experimental Theatre Club, which took up a great deal of her spare time. She went to dances and the cinema and parties, whenever possible with Paul Avery, an impecunious junior doctor at the Radcliffe Infirmary. Neither in character nor temperament did she bear any resemblance to Mary Rust or Kate Minden; all she had in common with them were her good looks.

At five o'clock on the day she went missing Linda was in the flat she shared with Paul when he was not on duty at the hospital. They had been very lucky to obtain what A. J. Knight's Estate Agency would have called a 'garden flat' in the basement of one of those large detached grey brick North Oxford houses, in which the front door and the ground floor were raised some steps above ground level, and the floors above included spacious bedrooms and attics.

Linda was brushing out her long blonde hair, which she

had just washed and dried, when the phone rang in the hall.
She rushed to answer it, expecting the call to be from Paul.
In fact, it was her tutor, Quentin Wood, at the other end of
the line.

'Come and have a drink at six, if you can,' he said.
'There's something I want to discuss with you.'

'Okay. I'll be along.'

There was no reason why she shouldn't keep the date.
Paul was not due till eight. Their supper was already prepared, needing only to be heated. The wine was cooling in
the small refrigerator in the kitchenette. The table was ready
laid, with candles and flowers, for this was a special occasion.
She had planned to put in some work on her next essay
before Paul arrived but, if Quentin Wood wanted to see her,
that could wait.

Wood lived no more than ten minutes' walk away, in a
quiet crescent off the Banbury Road, and shortly before six,
ignoring her bicycle, Linda set off on foot. She was fond of
Wood, was looking forward to having a drink with him and
was curious about his reason for this sudden invitation. Paul
had phoned as she was leaving, and she had promised to be
back well before eight.

She reached Wood's home and rang the bell. Wood
opened the door to her, took her coat and waved her to
the left of the hall into the booklined room he called his
workroom. Quentin Wood was forty-five. Twice divorced,
he continued to live in the house he had inherited from his
godfather, and in which he had brought up a son by his first
marriage and a daughter by his second. At present he lived
alone, with the help of a daily woman who came in to clean,
and he spent much of his time in the college of which he
was a Fellow. Someone had once remarked that, with his
coarse grey hair and his long face, he looked rather like a
donkey. There was some truth in this, but in reality he was
a clever man and a good tutor.

'Sherry, Linda?'

'Please.' She sat down in an armchair, legs tucked under her, and glanced idly around the room as she had done so many times before. At once she noticed something new— a photographic enlargement propped against a pile of books on Wood's desk. She got up again to examine it more closely. The subject surprised her slightly, but she couldn't resist a comment, 'Quentin, that's absolutely super,' she said.

The print was of a baby girl, naked except for a large bow of pink ribbon around her middle. She was lying on a cushion on her front, arms and legs spreadeagled, face turned towards the camera. Her expression, at once mischievous and knowing, made the photograph a parody of all the similarly embarrassing photographs of babies in similar attitudes commissioned by proud parents since the camera was invented.

'I'm glad you like it,' Wood said. 'I'm rather proud of it myself. One of my best efforts, if I may say so.'

'Who's the baby?' Linda asked.

'Ah, there's the rub. I have to admit I've got a grand-daughter. My son, following in my footsteps, married young. I only hope his marriage sticks better than mine did.'

Wood brought the sherry, and sat in an armchair opposite Linda. He lifted his glass to her. 'My dear, I have what I hope is good news for you. You know Winston Pearce?'

'I know of him. Who doesn't? After all, he's probably the leading UK political commentator these days,' Linda said immediately. 'That was a magnificent article he wrote for *The Economist* last week on the inevitable perpetuity of the so-called poverty trap.'

Wood nodded. 'He was dining at High Table in college a couple of weeks ago and we got talking. He's going to do a series of discussions on BBC television, with a different major figure each week and a small permanent panel of three. It's scheduled for transmission next spring, but he's getting it organized now. Anyway, he said he was looking for someone young, beautiful and intelligent, who could cope with that kind of situation. I thought of you at once, and your theatrical experience, apart from your other qualities, and I gave him your name.'

'Quentin! That's terrific! Thank you.'

'I thought you'd be pleased, Linda. There's no knowing what it might lead to or what contacts you might make. Pearce says he'll be in touch in a week or two when he gets back from the States; he wants to find an American for his panel.' Wood grinned at Linda, and picked up her glass. 'I think that deserves another sherry, don't you?'

Paul Avery carried his bicycle down the basement steps, padlocked it securely and felt for his keys. He was surprised that no lights were on, and that Linda hadn't come out to greet him. He opened the door and went into the hall, calling her name. There was no answer. It took him only a minute to assure himself that she was nowhere in the flat, and he swore softly.

He was not especially worried. Linda had said on the phone that she was going to have a drink with Quentin Wood, and Paul assumed that the tutor had delayed her. He expected her at any moment, and pictured her running down the basement steps, full of apologies for not being there when he arrived. Smiling to himself, he went into the kitchenette, put into the oven the casserole that Linda had prepared, together with the jacket potatoes which at the last moment he remembered to prick. He thought of cutting open the avocado, but decided against it. Instead, he poured himself a Cinzano and took it into the living-room.

He turned on the television. The nine o'clock news came and went. By now Paul was becoming annoyed. The evening had been intended as a celebration, but it was quite spoilt. He found Wood's number and dialled it, but there was no reply and he assumed that Linda had gone off somewhere with her tutor. He took the casserole and potatoes out of the oven, but although he was hungry, he couldn't bring himself to eat them alone. Instead, he settled for a beer and some bread and cheese.

Paul Avery was a sensible young man. As a junior hospital doctor he worked extremely hard, and had little free time. What he had he devoted to Linda. They made a good pair, he as dark as she was fair, and they were both looking forward to a happy life together. Paul couldn't understand how Linda could have deserted him on this of all nights. Not even a phone call, he thought with some bitterness.

This reminded him. He tried Wood's number again, and again there was no answer. But on his third or fourth attempt—he had lost count—he heard Quentin Wood's voice on the line. To Paul, the tutor sounded a little drunk.

'Linda? My dear chap, of course she's not here. Have you lost her?'

'When did she leave you?'

'I couldn't say exactly.' Wood had some trouble over the last word. 'Between seven-fifteen and seven-thirty, I think. Maybe a spot later. We had a lot to talk about, but she was anxious to get home and put a casserole in the oven, she said. You know, you're a lucky so-and-so, Paul Avery. You've got a girl in a million there.'

'And you've not seen her since about seven-thirty?' Paul had no time for exchanging banter. 'You've no idea where she might be? She didn't say she was going somewhere on her way home?'

'No, to all three questions, my dear boy. But, as to the last, she must have gone somewhere if she's not got home, mustn't she?'

'Yes. Well—thanks.'

Paul put down the receiver. He was now seriously worried. Linda could have been knocked down by a car, and be hurt or—or dead. Linda could have lost her memory, and gone God alone knew where. Linda could have been kidnapped, and her body would be found weeks later. Paul had read about Kate Minden and Mary Rust in the press, and though he found it hard to imagine their relevance to Linda, fear gripped him. If there was a maniac in the district . . .

He told himself not to panic. At least he knew where to make the obvious inquiries. He called the local hospitals that had casualty departments. The results were negative, and he didn't know whether or not to be thankful.

Next he tried the city police. They had no knowledge of Linda but they seemed to Paul to be unusually interested. He supposed this was because of the other two girls. He promised to see them in the morning if Linda hadn't reappeared by then.

But he couldn't just wait, go to bed and hope that when he woke up Linda would be beside him. He wrote a note saying that he was going to look for her, and would not be long, and propped it on the mantel where she was sure to see it if she returned first. Then, in his turn, he set off towards Quentin Wood's house.

He walked slowly. He peered down basement steps. If there was a drive he went in and looked behind bushes and dustbins, anywhere where Linda might be lying. The crescent where Wood lived was badly lit, and he searched it thoroughly. He thought of ringing Wood's bell, but decided there was nothing to be gained by this, so sadly he retraced his steps.

Linda had not returned. Paul tore up his note and flung it into the wastepaper basket. He was totally frustrated, with no idea what to do next. He could only face the fact that he must wait.

Because of the nature of his work Paul was used to going long hours without sleep and he didn't feel particularly tired now, although it was way after midnight. What he needed was something to occupy him, to help pass the time until he could take further action. He put on the kettle for tea and searched in the box where they stacked old newspapers for back copies of the *Oxford Mail*. Linda was inclined to hoard papers, and he soon found what he wanted.

He took the tea and the newspapers into the living-room. Five minutes later he was deeply immersed in the reports of the disappearance of Kate Minden, Mrs Katerina Minden, whose husband had recently been released from prison and had himself almost immediately disappeared. Next, he read about Mary Rust. Neither of the girls had yet been found, though in Mary's case the woods and fields around Colombury had been extensively and painstakingly searched. According to the press, the police considered it highly improbable that either Kate or Mary had gone missing of their own accord, and foul play was definitely suspected.

Paul Avery found little consolation in any of this, least of all in the pious hope expressed by a neighbour of the Rusts that, as things often happened in threes, a third girl would follow the first two into limbo. 'Not Linda,' he murmured under his breath. 'Please God, not Linda.'

Then a couple of lines caught his eye. Detective Chief Inspector Dick Tansey, who was in charge of the investigations, had said that so far there seemed to be no connection between the two cases, except that they had both taken place in the area covered by the Thames Valley Police. But it was Tansey's name, rather than his opinion, that interested Paul.

For Paul Avery knew Dick Tansey. To be precise he had met the Detective Chief Inspector three or four years ago, when Tansey—then merely an Inspector—had been investigating the death of a friend of Paul's, the son of a prominent politician, who had taken his own life while under the influence of drugs. Paul had found Tansey intelligent and understanding, and had been impressed by the way in which he had conducted the case. Now he seemed to Paul the ideal man to contact.

Leaping to his feet in a sudden burst of energy, Paul phoned the Thames Valley Police Headquarters in Kidlington, and demanded to speak to Tansey. He was informed that the Chief Inspector was not on duty, but if he would state his name and business—

Paul cut short the impersonal voice. He wanted Tansey and no one else. Eventually, he agreed to telephone again at 8.45 a.m. when it was expected that the Chief Inspector would be available.

Somehow Paul got through the rest of the night. The next morning he phoned Kidlington again, and this time he was lucky. Tansey was in his office, coping with a pile of paperwork. He was not too pleased to be interrupted, but he took the call. Paul identified himself, and reminded the Chief Inspector of the circumstances in which they had last met.

'Of course I remember,' Tansey said finally. 'What can I do for you now?'

'My fiancée, Linda Jackson, has disappeared, just—just like the other two girls the papers say you're trying to trace,' Paul said baldly.

'When? How?' The Chief Inspector's interest was aroused at once. He shot questions at Paul, which Paul did his best to answer.

'Okay,' said Tansey at last. 'The report of your phone call last night should be on my desk. I'll find it, and then be along. You can wait there?'

'Yes,' said Paul. 'I'm not on duty at the hospital till four.'

The Chief Inspector, he thought, as he slowly put down the receiver, had sounded efficient and businesslike, but obviously he hadn't yet been successful in finding Kate Minden or Mary Rust. While he waited, Paul wondered miserably how he would survive the prospect of never seeing Linda again.

CHAPTER 6

'I'm beginning to dislike weekends,' Detective Chief Inspector Tansey said meditatively. 'Come the weekend, and another young woman goes missing for no apparent reason. This is the third in so many weeks, Sergeant, and we're not getting anywhere in spite of a pretty massive effort.'

'I know, sir.' Hilary Greenway was sympathetic; she shared Tansey's frustration. 'At least this time we seem to have reliable witnesses and some definite times to work on. That might help.' She hooted as a car cut in sharply in front of her.

'It might, but—' Tansey sighed. 'This is the place, Sergeant. I gather Linda Jackson lives in the basement flat with her doctor boyfriend. And here is Dr Avery.'

Paul, who had heard their car draw up on the gravel drive, had come out of the flat and was standing at the bottom of the basement steps. He showed them in, and Tansey greeted him affably and introduced his sergeant. Paul recounted what he knew, and what he had done.

'We'll re-check with the hospitals and the local police,' Tansey said, 'and with Mr Wood. But for the moment we'll assume that Miss Jackson was fine at five forty-five when she spoke to you on the phone. Presumably she was equally fine when she left her tutor's house at seven-thirty or thereabouts. She should have reached home in ten minutes, you say. Are you sure she didn't, Doctor? Might she have returned and gone out again?'

'I hadn't thought of that,' Paul admitted. 'But why should she?' He cast an involuntary glance at the table, still laid for two, with its candles and flowers. 'She was expecting me.'

'You were going to celebrate something?' asked Sergeant Greenway.

'Er—yes. My birthday.'

'I'm afraid you didn't get a pleasant present then, Doctor,' Tansey said. 'Now, we'll need a photograph of Miss Jackson, and would you mind if Sergeant Greenway looked around your flat?'

'Of course not. Look around by all means, though I don't see what good it'll do. And I'll find you a photo.'

While Greenway was out of the room, Tansey asked a series of further questions about Linda, in an effort to establish her family background, her work and generally the kind of girl she was. 'Have you told her parents yet that she's missing?' he asked.

Paul shook his head. 'No. I suppose I must. I didn't want to worry them.'

'Well, Doctor, they'll have to know, if only to make sure she hasn't gone home, and doubtless it'll come better from you than from some police officer.' Tansey smiled wryly, then added, 'But we'll need their address. We'll have to see them, though that can wait. Meanwhile we'll try and keep it from the media for as long as we can—and as long as it's expedient to do so.'

'I see your point,' Paul said dully. 'I suppose publicity can help sometimes.' He mentally discarded the possibility that Linda had suddenly gone back to her home without leaving him some word, and he was not looking forward to breaking the news to her family.

Lost in thought, he missed Tansey's next question. 'Sorry. What did you say?'

'I asked about the people who live in the rest of the house. They may have seen Miss Jackson last night.'

For the first time Paul gave a genuine grin. 'When we came here an ancient professor and his wife owned the house, but they died within a few weeks of each other and a Miss Foyne inherited it; I think she and the professor's

wife were distantly related. Anyway, Miss Foyne lives there
now with her friend, another middle-aged spinster. They're
a funny old pair, but kind enough. Fortunately, this flat is
completely self-contained, so we hardly ever come across
them, but I suppose they might have seen Linda.'

'How long have you been here?' Tansey asked.

'A year and a bit. We came shortly before the professor
died,' Paul said. 'And I may say we were jolly lucky to get
the place. It was pure accident.'

The two men ceased talking as Greenway returned. She
smiled at Paul. 'I can see preparations had been made for
your dinner. What about the casserole, which has been
horribly overcooked? Did you find it in the oven?'

'No. Linda had got everything else ready, so I put it in
when I came home. I thought Wood had kept Linda and
she'd be back any minute. Then I forgot it, and when I took
it out I realized I couldn't face it alone. I never even looked
inside, so I didn't know it was overcooked.'

'A pity,' said Tansey, 'like so much else about this case.
That's all for the moment, Doctor. We'll go now, but we'll
be in touch. At the moment, to be frank, I can't offer you
any encouragement. However, I don't need to tell you that
we'll do everything we can.'

'Yes. Thank you,' Paul muttered.

He saw the two officers out, going up the basement steps
with them. A small square woman with fluffy white hair
was tending the plants which grew in pots on either side of
the main front door of the house, which was raised five or
six stone steps above ground level. She looked up when she
heard them, and smiled.

Paul glanced inquiringly at Tansey, who nodded. Paul
took the cue. 'Miss Gower,' he said, 'were you and Miss
Foyne at home yesterday evening?'

'Most of the time, yes. Why, Dr Avery?'

'Did you see Miss Jackson go out about six o'clock, or
come home later?'

Miss Gower put her head on one side as if this question required a great deal of thought. 'No,' she said at last. 'You know that our sitting-room looks over the garden at the back, so we rarely see anyone. I never saw Miss Jackson yesterday at all. Is it important? Shall I ask Miss Foyne?'

Without waiting for an answer, Miss Gower bustled into the house. Paul took the opportunity to say to Tansey, 'Was that what you wanted? This is all a bit embarrassing. Shouldn't I introduce you?'

Tansey shook his head. 'Not at this stage,' he said. 'You're doing fine. Let's not start any unnecessary rumours.'

Miss Gower came back almost at once. 'No. Miss Foyne never saw her yesterday either.' She regarded Paul Avery and the two detectives with faded but sharp blue eyes. 'Has something happened to her? Oh, I do hope not. She's such a beautiful young lady.'

'No, Miss Gower, there's nothing to worry about,' Paul said quickly. 'I'll wait to hear from you,' he added to Tansey, and ran down the basement steps.

Miss Gower looked vaguely puzzled as Sergeant Greenway opened the car door for the Chief Inspector, but she returned to her plants without comment. 'To Mr Wood's now, sir?' Greenway asked as she got in behind the wheel.

Tansey nodded. 'When you were riffling through the flat did anything else strike you, Sergeant, apart from the dried-up casserole?'

'Well, sir, I know this sounds pretty stupid, but it did strike me that the doctor was a little diffident about his birthday celebration.'

'I noticed that, too,' Tansey admitted, 'but heaven knows if it signifies anything.'

Sergeant Greenway drove slowly along the road until she reached Quentin Wood's address. At night the crescent was 'a place of long dark shadows, but by day it was most attractive.

The housekeeper opened the door of Wood's large house to the two officers. At first she was unwilling to let them in. Mr Wood was still in bed and was not to be disturbed. However, when the Chief Inspector gave his name and insisted, she showed the two officers into the booklined room where Linda had talked with Wood the previous evening. They had only a short time to wait before Wood appeared, his grey hair rumpled and his face unshaven, but with white silk pyjama trousers showing below a scarlet robe.

'This is a disgusting time to call on a man,' he said, 'or a woman for that matter. What have I done to deserve it? Or has someone pinched my car?' He sounded suddenly anxious.

'Not as far as I know,' said Tansey casually. 'It's Miss Linda Jackson we've come about. We believe she visited you yesterday evening.'

'Linda? Yes, that's true.' At last Wood waved them to chairs. 'She came at six, had a couple of sherries and left about seven-thirty. I told Dr Avery, her boyfriend, all that when he phoned last night.'

'So he said, sir. Unfortunately it seems that she never reached home after she left here.'

'Good God! You don't mean she's disappeared—like those other girls?' Wood was horrified. 'But she was sensible, not some fool who'd take a lift from a strange man. Besides, she lives no more than ten minutes' walk from here.'

'You actually saw her to the door?' Tansey asked. 'Which way did she go?'

'To the right, fractionally the quickest way out of this crescent. She didn't have her bike. She was on foot.' Wood frowned, as if trying to reconstruct the scene. 'I'm sorry, but that's all I can tell you. I don't remember noticing anyone about, either walking or in a car of any kind. Linda went off perfectly happily.'

'Apart from Dr Avery and yourself, would anyone have known she was going to call on you yesterday evening, sir?'

'No. It was an impulse on my part,' Wood said. 'I'd just been speaking to Winston Pearce on the phone, and he'd confirmed something we'd talked about earlier. I decided to give Linda the good news there and then.' Wood told them about Pearce's BBC project, and Linda's delight at the prospect. 'She was over the moon, as they insist on saying these days. Her eyes were positively shining with excitement. She's a beautiful girl, Chief Inspector—one of those rare natural blondes—and Paul Avery's a lucky man. I can't believe that—Chief Inspector, if she's gone missing, I'd swear it was not of her own free will.'

'No one seems to believe it was voluntary, sir. That's why we're investigating the matter.' Tansey paused. 'You went out yourself later?'

'Shortly before eight, yes. I went to visit a friend, a lady friend.' He grinned. 'Naturally I wasn't thinking about Linda, but I didn't see anything untoward on my way through the crescent.'

Wood glanced at his watch. Over the years he had had a great deal of practice at indicating with economy and politeness that his time was precious, and that the present tutorial, or interview, or whatever, was at an end. The Chief Inspector took the hint, and rose obediently. He thanked Wood for his help and, followed by Sergeant Greenway, took his leave. Standing in the doorway in his flamboyant night attire, Quentin Wood watched them drive away.

'So what did you think of him, Sergeant?' Tansey asked.

'Clever. Rather patronizing. I didn't like him much.'

'He liked you. Surely you noticed his eyes on your legs?'

Hilary Greenway laughed. The Chief Inspector was mellowing, she thought. A week ago he would never have mentioned her legs in that way. But she merely asked, 'Where to now, sir?' as they reached the main road.

'Kidlington,' Tansey said immediately. 'We'll pay another call on those estate agents. I'm not totally happy about Mr Peter Cousin. He could so easily have driven Kate

Minden into the country somewhere. There's no proof he dropped her by the Randolph—or that he waited at this house he was hoping to sell. You told me yourself the supposed clients swear their appointment was for Saturday, not Friday.'

'That's right, sir. And there's no news of Kate's husband yet, I see,' Greenway remarked.

'No, unfortunately not, in spite of all our best efforts,' Tansey said. 'He's probably in some doss house, and we can guess what he'll say when we do find him—never seen a paper, so he doesn't know she's missing. But I wish he'd turn up. We might be able to eliminate him.'

There was a new girl sitting behind Kate Minden's desk in Knight's Estate Agency. She was varnishing her nails, and seemed less than pleased by the interruption. 'Yes?' she snapped.

'Is Mr Cousin in?' Tansey asked, without identifying himself or his companion.

'No!'

'When will he be back?'

'No idea.' She finished with her left hand, regarded it with admiration, and started on the right. 'I'm only a Temp here,' she volunteered.

'What about Mr Knight?'

'What about him?'

Tansey restrained himself with difficulty. 'Is *he* in?'

'No. He's not in either.'

'Maybe I can help, Chief Inspector.' Peter Cousin opened the front door and limped into the office. He grinned at Sergeant Greenway. 'We're keeping Kate's job open for her, as you see. We live in hopes.'

'We'd like a few words with you, Mr Cousin, if it's convenient,' Tansey replied politely.

'Come into the inner sanctum.' The Temp had pricked up her ears at the mention of the Chief Inspector's rank, and she stared at them curiously as Cousin led them into the small rear office and shut the door firmly. 'Not quite soundproof,' he said, 'but I somehow doubt if our Temp will be interested enough to listen. She doesn't seem interested in anything much. Now, what can I do for you?'

'First, will you tell us where you were last night between five and ten?' Tansey said.

'Last night? Between five and ten?' Cousin seemed to find the question difficult. 'You mean Friday night?'

'That's right, Mr Cousin.'

'Well, I can't see that it matters, but I was here until five-thirty. Then I had a whisky and lemon in the pub along the road and went home. I watched the box and went to bed early. I thought I was starting a cold.'

'It doesn't seem to have materialized,' Sergeant Greenway said.

'The cold? No, luckily not. Maybe the whisky helped.'

Tansey said, 'You live in Oxford, don't you? St John's Road, isn't it?'

'Yes. I've got a bedsitter there. I wash in one cupboard and cook in another and share the communal bathroom,' Cousin replied. 'It's not as bad as it sounds. It's a good, big room. Perhaps I should tell you that I also own a cottage in the Cotswolds, not far from Colombury.' Peter Cousin added his last sentence a little tentatively.

There was an appreciable silence while the three of them thought of Mary Rust. Then Tansey said, 'Are you trying to tell us something, Mr Cousin?'

'Only about the cottage. And yes, before you ask, I was there the Saturday the Rust girl disappeared. I imagine you probably know that already, or if not you'll find out sooner rather than later, and assume the worst.' Cousin stuck out his chin, and regarded Tansey aggressively. 'But I know nothing about Rust. Frankly I don't care a damn about her. But Kate—Kate's different.' His voice suddenly grew husky and he couldn't continue.

'How different, Mr Cousin?' Greenway asked softly.

'She—she wouldn't have looked at me,' Cousin said, 'but I loved her—love her. I wouldn't have hurt her, not for anything in the world.'

'Poor man,' Hilary Greenway commented as she drove away from the office.

'Maybe.' Tansey remained dubious. 'Did you notice how he corrected himself, Sergeant? He said he *loved* Kate—past tense—and altered it to *love*, as though to make it look as if he believed she was still alive. And he has no alibi for last night. He could be our man. Mind, I'm not saying he is, but he's certainly a possible. I suspect he's got some kind of chip on his shoulder because of that limp, and he might have gone round the bend.'

'I'd still say, "Poor man," sir,' Greenway said.

'Not if he's done away with three girls,' the Chief Inspector said firmly, surprised at the sentimental view taken by his sergeant. 'And we don't want any more. It's a hell of nuisance that we don't have the resources to put Cousin under round-the-clock surveillance.'

CHAPTER 7

'I screwed her. She'd never been screwed before, and I hurt her and frightened her. There was a lot of blood and—and she just didn't understand.'

Brian Quayle broke down. He folded his arms on the bare wooden table in what passed for an interrogation room in the Colombury Police Station, and buried his head in them. His face was wet with tears, and his great shoulders heaved with dry sobs. He was as scared as Mary Rust had been.

Sergeant Court had gone along to the butchers where Brian worked, and had demanded that Brian accompany

him. Brian was busy—at that moment trimming the excess
fat off a leg of lamb for a customer in a hurry—and Brian's
employer had objected that he couldn't spare his assistant
on a Saturday morning, not with so many people wanting
to buy their Sunday joint. But Sergeant Court had been
adamant. Detective Chief Inspector Tansey needed to see
Brian now, not in a couple of hours' time, and as far as he
was concerned that was the end of the matter.

And when Brian had arrived at the police station, red-
faced and apprehensive, Tansey's questions had been harsh.
He accused Brian of lying about the Saturday afternoon he
had spent with Mary Rust. For one thing, Brian had returned the motorbike he had borrowed much later than he
had claimed.

'What were you doing during that time?' Tansey had
demanded. 'Burying Mary's body in Copley Wood?'

'No! No! I never killed her. I loved her,' Brian had said
desperately as he started to weep.

'Another thwarted lover,' Tansey had muttered to Greenway.

But Brian hadn't been thwarted. Through his tears he
explained how he had taken Mary into the wood and made
love to her, that she had seemed to enjoy the preliminaries,
and that by the time she had started to become frightened
he had been unable to stop. It was a very common—and a
very human—tale, thought Hilary Greenway to herself.

At Tansey's request Sergeant Court brought tea, and after
the youth had drunk a strong cup liberally laced with sugar,
the Chief Inspector took him through his story again. By
this time Brian Quayle had regained control of his emotions,
so much so as to seem slightly embarrassed at Hilary's
presence during some of the more intimate questions.

'Okay,' Tansey said, as Brian stopped speaking. 'You
rolled off Mary. What then?'

'She had started to cry,' Brian said. 'There was blood,
which as far as I could tell she hadn't expected, and more

than I'd expected for that matter. She'd been hard to break into. I guessed she was a virgin, but I'd never—' Brian could find no more words.

Tansey waited and then said gently, 'Well?'

'I gave her my hankie to mop herself up a bit. Hers was only a scrap and no use at all. She'd stood up, but I lay on my back and watched her. I didn't want to make a great thing of it.' Brian was gaining in confidence. 'Well, then, suddenly, without any warning, she stamped her foot. "I hate you, Brian Quayle," she said. "I hate you," and she ran off. God knows where she went. I've not seen her since, and that's the truth.'

'I assume you didn't just leap on your bike and forget her,' Tansey said. 'You went to look for her.'

'Of course, and I called her name and shouted. But there was no sign of her, and at last I gave up. I'd heard a car not long after she ran off, and I thought perhaps she'd got a lift back into Colombury. I—I was absolutely shook when Betty told me she'd not got home and old Rust was on the warpath.'

'You heard this car? You didn't see it?'

'No, sir.'

'Did you see anyone at all while you were in the wood?'

'No, but—but Mary got a bit uneasy once. She said she was sure someone was watching us through the bushes. I thought she was trying to slow me down, and I told her not to be silly, but I suppose there could have been a Peeping Tom or something.'

The Chief Inspector hid his interest. He was at least ninety per cent certain that Brian Quayle had finally told the truth, and this was a new twist. He checked the time.

'Right,' he said. 'We'll take you out to Copley Wood, and you can show us exactly where you were with Mary.'

In the event, the expedition achieved little except that Tansey was able to direct the attention of the scene of crime inspector, whose men were still busy searching the wood, to the clearing where Brian and Mary had made love, and to that part of the wood nearest to the road.

Walking back to their police car, Sergeant Greenway said casually, 'Did you go to the disco last night, Brian?'

'Last night? Yes,' he said, startled by the question. 'Why do you ask, miss?'

'I just wondered.'

'I didn't much want to go, to be honest, but my dad said I ought because it was what I usually did,' Brian admitted. 'And it wasn't as if I ever went dancing with Mary. She wasn't allowed,' he added gloomily.

'So you spent the evening at the disco?'

'That's right. I got there at eight, and left at twelve. Four wretched hours, pretending I was enjoying myself and all the time . . .'

Brian lapsed into a disconsolate silence, while the Chief Inspector exchanged glances with his sergeant. This time they had no doubt that Brian was telling the truth; it would be too simple to check on the time he had arrived at the dance. And if he had been in Colombury at 8.00 p.m., he couldn't possibly have been anywhere near Quentin Wood's house in Oxford at 7.30. So as far as Linda Jackson was concerned he was in the clear. What was more, there had never been any real substance to the idea that he might have been involved in Kate Minden's disappearance—or evidence to support any such theory.

They dropped Brian back at the butchers' shop, where a small queue eyed them curiously, and drove on to Tenworth, a village on the far side of Colombury from Copley Wood. Peter Cousin had given them directions, and they found his cottage without difficulty. When they reached it they realized why he had been cynically amused by their request to inspect the place.

The cottage was nearly at the end of the village, but in no way isolated. It had a minute front garden, and a much larger back garden, both completely overlooked. In the short time they were there Cousin's next door neighbour hastened to tell them that Mr Cousin was not at home, a woman pushing a pram inspected them with great care and a clergyman on a bicycle stopped to ask if he could help them. True, the curtains at the rear of the cottage were closely drawn, but it was hard to imagine Peter Cousin carrying an unconscious woman up his garden path without every villager knowing within minutes.

'There's nothing for us here,' Tansey said. 'Perhaps Cousin could smuggle a girl into his cottage in the middle of a midwinter snowstorm, or on a dark, rainy night, without anyone knowing, but even then I've got my doubts.'

Greenway laughed. 'Don't forget they go to bed early in these parts, sir,' she said. Tansey gave her a cold stare, and she wished that her riposte hadn't sounded quite so smart and casual.

It was 5.00 p.m. the same evening. Dick Tansey was sitting at his desk and regarding his half-empty in-tray with satisfaction. At least he had dealt with the routine stuff. Idly he wondered why senior police officers seemed to suffer from more and more unnecessary paperwork. He knew that in forty-eight hours the tray would again be piled high.

He yawned and stretched. It had been a long, unsatisfactory day—especially unsatisfactory, of course, because of the disappearance of the third girl, Linda Jackson. He wished he had never been given the case—or cases—in the first place. He had made so little progress that he couldn't decide whether he was meant to be dealing with one, or two, or even three, separate files.

Unless they were dealing with a psychopath—and he kept that thought firmly at the back of his mind—he could see no apparent connection between the three young women. They came from differing backgrounds, had been leading quite different kinds of lives and had disappeared in different circumstances. The one thing that seemed certain—and even this could only be supposition—was that none of them had gone missing willingly. Kate Minden would never have deserted the child to whom she was apparently so devoted. A check on transport had suggested that, unless she had accepted a lift, Mary Rust had never left the vicinity of Colombury and, except perhaps under extreme stress, a girl like that would be too timid to get into a car with a stranger. As for Linda Jackson, she was apparently enjoying a rewarding present and was looking forward to a future full of promise; why should she wish to abandon all this voluntarily?

This was speculation, Tansey thought. What was needed was evidence—hard evidence. Resignedly he forced himself to concentrate on the remaining piles of paper in front of him. He still had to prepare an initial report on the Jackson case, and to update his earlier reports on Minden and Rust. Inquiries were continuing all over the country, naturally, and a great deal of time, both of police personnel and of computer back-up, was being devoted to the three girls. The results of this activity were mostly useless, but they had to be read and studied before the reports could be written.

On that Saturday, it appeared that Kate Minden had been seen in places as far apart as Edinburgh and Frome, and someone was sure she had seen Mary Rust with a tall, dark man at London Airport. Every one of the so-called sightings had been checked, and found false.

Tansey was more interested in the fact that for the second time a man had telephoned Police Headquarters at Kidlington, asking if a reward was being offered for information concerning Katerina Minden. That he had called Kate by her full name was intriguing in itself. Tansey made a note to the effect that if the man called again, he was to be told that there would be a reward commensurate with the value of the information he offered.

The Chief Inspector started to draft his report. He kept

it brief, and had almost completed it when there was a tap at his door. Sergeant Greenway came in.

'One or two items, sir.'

'I hope they don't mean I'll have to rewrite any of this.'

'I shouldn't think so, sir, though one might be of some importance.'

Tansey leaned back in his chair, and indicated that Greenway should sit opposite him. 'Right. What have you got?'

'First, yesterday was *not* Dr Avery's birthday. Whatever he and Linda Jackson were preparing to celebrate it wasn't that. I looked him up in the *Medical Directory*, and he was born in May.'

Tansey nodded. He was accustomed to witnesses telling the oddest untruths, and for no apparent reason. 'We'll have to ask him about that. What else?'

'A lady telephoned—I have her name and address—to say that on the Friday Kate disappeared she saw a girl who might have been Kate at the bus stop by Christ Church. A car drew up beside her, and the supposed Kate got in and they drove off.'

'Usual questions,' said Tansey briskly. 'How definite was your lady? What descriptions could she give? Why hasn't she come forward before?'

'She's sure of the date because she was going to spend the night with a friend in Abingdon, and they were driving down to Devon together the next day. That answers your last question too, sir. They were touring around, and didn't bother with newspapers or TV. Curiously enough these days, they had no car radio,' Greenway added. 'I asked specially.'

Tansey nodded his approval. 'You said she was going to Abingdon. Would she have been catching what we might call Kate's bus?'

'Yes, sir, but she was on the other side of the road when the car drew up. She was waiting to cross to the bus stop.'

'Or she might have disappeared too,' Tansey murmured.

'I doubt it, sir. She described herself as a sixty-year-old, grey-haired granny, and she sounded too sensible to take lifts from strangers. I thought I'd go to see her tomorrow with a photo of Kate, if you agree, sir.'

'Yes. You may be able to prod her memory.' Tansey was thoughtful. 'Go on.'

'Her description of the girl fitted Kate pretty well. What she remembered best was the long red hair. But she fell down over the car, sir. She said it was just an ordinary car, either blue or green, she wasn't sure which.'

'Damn!' Tansey said. 'How typical of a woman to concentrate on the colour and not the make. And she couldn't even get the colour right. Pity it wasn't a man.'

'If it had been a man he'd have probably been so busy looking at Kate that he wouldn't have noticed anything at all about the vehicle, sir.'

'You think so, Sergeant? Well, let's agree it's a pity the witness wasn't a small boy. He'd have noted the make and probably the registration number too.'

'Yes, sir,' Greenway said meekly. She hesitated, and added, 'I still find it hard to believe that Kate would have accepted a lift from a *total* stranger. An acquaintance, perhaps?'

'Who owns a blue or green car. That leaves a fairly wide field.' Nevertheless, Tansey was interested. 'But it could be a lead. Brian Quayle mentioned hearing a car just after Mary Rust ran off. In her state she might easily have jumped at any chance to escape from Copley Wood. But Linda Jackson had only a few minutes' walk—she'd hardly have needed a lift, and in any case it's stretching coincidence to the extreme to accept that she and Kate Minden had an acquaintance in common.'

'You've reached the conclusion the three disappearances are connected, sir?'

'No, I certainly haven't. It's contrary to all reason and common sense. And yet . . .' Tansey shook his head sadly.

'Somehow I've a hunch they're connected.'

'May I say something, sir?'

'Go ahead. You're not usually so bashful, Sergeant.'

'Well, the obvious conclusion is that the three had nothing in common—background, interests, friends and so on. There's even a ten-year age gap between Kate and Mary. Yet there is one characteristic they did share.' Greenway was warming to her theme, and paused as if to emphasize the point she was about to make. 'They were all beautiful —and I don't mean merely pretty. Re-reading my notes, I see how in each case people commented on their beauty, as if it were unusual, out of the ordinary. I doubt if the photographs we have of them do them justice, sir, except perhaps Peter Cousin's prints of Kate. And from their descriptions we know that none of them were big girls. They were all of medium height, with slender figures and lovely long hair. Maybe it's irrelevant, but—'

Hilary Greenway stopped talking and looked defiantly at the Chief Inspector. If he laughs at me, I shall throw something at him, she thought. But Tansey didn't laugh.

He said, 'Don't think I'm trying to steal your idea, Sergeant, but I must admit that somewhat the same thought has been at the back of my mind, though I've never put it into words—let alone a report. Because if it's relevant, as it might be, we've probably got someone to deal with who's mentally unbalanced. That's a possibility all right, though not a happy one. And whether or not it reduces the chances of finding any of the girls still alive I wouldn't know.'

CHAPTER 8

Dick Tansey had decided to take the next day—Sunday— off duty; the single day represented a fraction of the free time to which he was entitled. In any case, he would be at home and available should he be needed urgently.

He got up late, had breakfast in his dressing-gown and read the Sunday papers. As usual they were full of wars and rumours of wars, political scandals and corruption, appeals for charity and artful tear-jerking stories; even the sports pages were tainted. Tansey was not pleased to see that the disappearance of Linda Jackson, described as a glorious ash-blonde with violet eyes, had been made the focus for an attack on the efficiency of the Thames Valley Police. The Chief Constable, he thought, would have something to say about that—and probably to him personally.

Throwing aside the papers, he had a rudimentary wash and shave just in case his presence were demanded in a hurry, but he put on old clothes. He went into the garden. He was not an expert gardener, but he enjoyed caring for his small patch, and firmly believed that the exercise kept him trim. This was a fallacy; he was the type of man who would always remain lean.

He spent the morning toiling, and shortly before noon returned to the house, where he had a shower and put on some more respectable garments. Then he went into the kitchen. After his wife had walked out he had taught himself to cook, and now took some pleasure in the art. He prepared a pheasant casserole for his dinner, which could be re-heated and would last for several meals, and then made himself a mushroom omelette and a mixed salad for lunch. He was finishing his cheese when the telephone rang.

'Sergeant Greenway here, sir. I'm sorry to disturb you, but the man who wanted to know if there was a reward for information about Kate Minden has phoned again. He's prepared to talk. According to him, it's worth a hundred quid—that's how he puts it, sir. But he insists on talking to you, and you alone. No one else will do, he says, because you're the bloke in charge.'

'Okay,' Tansey said without hesitation. 'Where does he want to meet?'

'He'll be at the Black Boar on the Oxford Road at opening time this evening. He says you can stand him a double whisky, sir.'

'Does he indeed? Has he got a name?'

'He refused to give one, but he'll have a flower in his buttonhole so you'll recognize him. It sounds like something from a spy tale, sir. Or it could be a trap of some kind. Shall I come with you?'

'No, I don't think that will be necessary, Sergeant. I've an idea who he might be, and I think I'll recognize him, with or without a flower. He shouldn't be dangerous. Anything else fresh?'

'I interviewed the lady who thinks she saw Kate outside Christ Church. She's a sensible woman. She wouldn't swear to the photograph I showed her, but she's pretty sure it was the same girl. That's all. Nothing more on the car; she simply didn't notice it.'

'At least that's an improvement on making something up, even if it's not exactly helpful,' Tansey said, still regretting the lack of a description of the vehicle.

'And I managed to contact Dr Avery. I went to his flat, but he wasn't there. However, that funny old duck, Miss Gower, was feeding her plants again, and she said he was probably at the hospital. She let me use their phone. Dr Avery was *not* helpful. He agreed that it wasn't his birthday that he and Linda had been about to celebrate, but he said the real reason was none of our business. We could better spend our time trying to find Linda, as well as the other girls.'

'Poor devil,' said Tansey after a pause. 'Perhaps he's right.'

The Black Boar was already open when the Chief Inspector arrived. There were half a dozen people standing around the bar, and a young couple sitting on an oak settle by the wall, holding hands. Tansey ordered half a pint of bitter and took it to a corner table, as if he were expecting friends. Five minutes later a man with a slightly-wilted rose in the lapel of his jacket walked in.

The newcomer was big, with black hair and vivid blue eyes, but there was an unmistakable unhealthy pallor about his skin, and his brown suit did nothing for him. Nevertheless, he glanced about the bar with an assumed air of casual arrogance, then walked over to Tansey, put his two hands on the table and leant towards the Chief Inspector. His breath stank of liquor.

'You the bloke who's interested in Katerina?' he asked softly.

'That's right,' said Tansey non-committally. 'What'll you drink?'

'Whisky, neat—a double, seeing as it's on the taxpayer.' He grinned, showing deep dimples in his cheeks and reminding Tansey of a film star whose name he failed to remember.

Tansey went across to the bar and got the whisky. The man drank it in silence. Tansey had scarcely touched his beer. Immediately the man pushed his empty glass across to Tansey.

'Same again,' he said, 'only this time with equal soda.'

Tansey collected the drink without comment, returned and planted it in front of his companion. Then he said, gently but firmly, 'Now talk!'

'There's no hurry.' The man lay back in his chair. 'Don't you want to know how I recognized you as the bloke bringing me that lovely bread?'

'No,' said Tansey, 'but I expect you're going to tell me.'

The man said sourly, 'I can smell a pig a mile off.'

Tansey said casually, 'I can smell something, too—an ex-con who's not reported to his probation officer recently.'

The man looked slightly abashed, but only slightly. 'So what,' he said. 'All I've done is miss a couple of meetings; that could be put right in a minute. D'you think they'd put me inside again for something like that—with the places as full as they are? You must be joking. Anyway, you set your dogs on me and I won't talk at all. Which is it to be?'

Tansey thought to himself, it's not quite as simple as that, my friend, but he merely said, 'Let's get down to business.'

The man said, 'I thought you'd see it my way. Okay. How much? It's worth a hundred smackers.'

'I'll decide how much when I hear what you've got to say.'

The man regarded him with a jaundiced expression, then seemed to reach a decision. 'Do you read porno magazines?' he asked suddenly. 'I bet you do. You're not married, are you?'

'Not at the moment,' Tansey said.

'Ah! She walked out on you, did she? You and me both.' The whisky, on top of what he had already drunk, was beginning to work on him. 'We should have a fellow feeling.'

'Sure,' Tansey said. 'And now let's stop making believe this is a social occasion, Mr Minden. What's a porno magazine got to do with Katerina?'

'You know who I am?'

'Mr Minden, you're not as dumb as that. You heard what I said about an ex-con just now. Do you think I've not seen your mug shot? Anyway, I suspected it would be you even before we met—'

'Okay. Okay. Forget it. As for Katerina and porno mags, that's what she's doing now—posing for them. I always knew she was a whore.' From the inside pocket of his jacket he produced what was obviously the colour centre spread from a glossy magazine. 'Take a gander at that.'

Tansey studied the pictures. He had seen many such before when he had served a tour on the Vice Squad, but these were particularly lewd and obscene. True, the model had a beautiful body, but she had been posed in positions that were revolting and degrading; in another context some might have been called almost gynæcological. Tansey was disgusted by them, but he hid his disgust—and his disappointment.

'Why do you say that's Katerina?' he asked. 'A lot of girls have long hair, and the face is practically hidden in all those shots. I suppose it might be her, but equally it might not.'

'Of course it's her. Don't you think I know my own wife?' He thumped his fist on the table, causing the landlord of the Black Boar, who was serving behind the bar, to regard him with some concern.

'That's Katerina, I tell you. Look at that one!' He pointed a bitten fingernail at the colour print on the back page of the fold.

The Chief Inspector looked—and looked again. The photograph was of the girl, naked but for a large bow of pink ribbon around her waist. She was on all fours. Her head was turned towards the camera, but her hair was brushed forward and, reaching to the floor, concealed most of her face. Her buttocks were raised, invitingly. There was no need for any interpretation.

'You say this is your wife?' Tansey said, as if in doubt. The photograph reminded him of something he had seen recently, but he couldn't place it immediately.

'It *is* my wife, I tell you!' Minden was growing angry. He thumped the table again, making the glasses bounce. He pointed to the girl's right buttock. 'See that pinkish mark? It's what they call a strawberry mark. Kate's had it from birth. They usually go away quite early in life, I think, but Kate's has kind of grown with her. How many other girls in Britain have got a mark like that right there? None, I bet you. So don't tell me that isn't Katerina.'

'All right, I won't. You've convinced me, Mr Minden,' said Tansey. Though he couldn't reconcile the girl in the picture with what he had learnt from other sources of the caring, conscientious Kate, he was speaking the truth. Certainly he was sure that Minden was not deliberately lying, and he wondered if Kate had chosen to prostitute herself—he could think of no other word to describe posing in such a fashion—because of her obsession with making money for the child, Zelda.

Then he dismissed the idea. If she had wished to do so, Kate could have got a much better job than the one she had with Knight's Estate Agency. She had deliberately chosen it for its obscurity, so that Minden would be unlikely to trace her, and for its proximity to Abingdon. Would she prejudice this anonymity by indulging in such a part-time occupation? There was one step that must certainly be taken, he reflected—and at once.

Affecting a cheerfulness he didn't feel, Tansey said, 'Well, I think that deserves another drink, don't you?'

'What about the money?' Minden said. 'What I've told you—what I've given you—is worth a hundred quid at least.'

'Sure,' said Tansey. 'It's very valuable information. I'll be back in a moment.'

Minden didn't try to stop him, and Tansey went up to the bar. He stood so that Minden couldn't see what he was doing and, as he extracted a note from his wallet, he brought out a card on which were his name, rank and an emergency phone number at the Kidlington Headquarters. When the landlord came to serve him he asked for a double whisky.

'Your friend's had about enough,' the publican said doubtfully. 'More than enough, if you ask me.'

'Yes,' Tansey said. 'Phone quickly but discreetly, please,' he murmured, pushing the card across the bar as he paid with the note. There was no time to explain or pass any message before he pocketed his change. When the publican nodded imperceptibly, the Chief Inspector picked up Minden's drink and raised his voice. 'Thanks a lot.'

'You've been a long time,' Minden said suspiciously as Tansey set the whisky in front of him.

'They're getting busy now,' Tansey said mildly. He saw the landlord say something to the girl who was serving with him, and then go into a room behind the bar. Tansey glanced at his watch. Ten minutes at most, he thought. He said, 'Why didn't you come forward before, Mr Minden? You've been free some while.'

Minden seemed surprised by the question. 'Why should I? I didn't know where she was, and I didn't care. Then I happened to see this mag, and the idea occurred to me that my info might be worth a bit. You could have had it before, if you'd been a bit less bloody tight-fisted.'

'And there's nothing else you can tell me?' Tansey was playing for time.

'What more do you want? You can see the name of the mag—*Beautiful Butterflies*. Katerina's become a beautiful butterfly. If you can't trace her through that you're even less efficient than I thought.' Minden's speech was becoming slurred. 'So give me my hundred quid and I'll be off. I don't like consorting with pigs more than I have to. Oh, and you can tell your chums I'll fix everything with my probation officer.'

It won't be as simple as that, thought Tansey again. He said, 'I don't have a hundred.'

'What? But you agreed! How much have you got?'

'Twenty-five.'

'Twenty-five! Bloody rubbish! A hundred, that's what they said.' Minden thumped the table again. 'Never trust a pig. Seventy-five, then.'

Tansey shook his head. Out of the corner of his eye he had seen a police car draw up outside the Black Boar. Two uniformed officers leapt out, and made for the door of the pub. If only I could have got a message to them to use an unmarked car and approach discreetly, Tansey thought, and that was all he had time to think before he felt the edge of the table slammed into his stomach. Minden too had spotted the police car.

The next few minutes were chaos. Minden was on his feet. He had seized Tansey's beer glass, smashed off its rim and was using it as a weapon. He attacked Tansey first, attempting to thrust the jagged glass into the Chief Inspector's head.

There was little Tansey could do to protect himself. He was pinned against the wall by the table and badly winded, but he threw up his right arm to save his face and did his best to fling himself sideways. He felt the bite of the glass on his hand and wrist. Then, as the pressure against his body was relaxed, he lost his balance and slid to the ground.

Above him Minden fought. Tansey, struggling to extricate himself from the table and the chair on which he had been sitting so that he could stand up, heard the crash of more glass and the splintering of wood. Suddenly he was aware of someone helping him, and a face near his.

'What the hell are you doing here?' he said.

'I was at HQ when the call came through and—You've hurt your hand, sir.' Hilary Greenway was glad of the opportunity to change the subject.

'He got me with a broken glass. Lucky it wasn't my eyes,' Tansey said, pulling out a handkerchief and binding it tightly round his hand to staunch the bleeding.

By now Minden had been subdued. Handcuffed, he was being frog-marched out of the bar by the two police officers. At the door he turned and spewed forth a flood of expletives directed at Tansey. The landlord, helped by some of his less shocked customers, had begun to set the place to rights.

'Sorry about the mess,' Tansey said.

'That's all right, sir. It's not much, and I'm insured against damage. If the insurers don't pay, I guess the police will.' The publican grinned philosophically at the Chief Inspector. 'It doesn't often happen here, this sort of thing,' he said.

One of the uniformed officers returned, with a swelling under his right eye. 'Are you all right, sir?' he asked anxiously and, when Tansey nodded, he added, 'He's a nasty customer, that one. What shall we charge him with? Assault?'

'No. Just drunk and disorderly, for the moment. Then throw him in a cell and let him stew overnight. I'll deal with him in the morning. Incidentally, he's an ex-con called Steve Minden, and we've been looking for him for a week or so.'

'Very good, sir. You have your car? Or do you want a lift?'

'I've got my car, thanks.'

The officer glanced briefly, very briefly, at Sergeant Greenway, saluted the Chief Inspector, and departed. The landlord came across to them, carrying two glasses.

'A brandy, sir, for you and the young lady. On the house.'

They thanked him, though neither of them wanted the liquor. They drank it as quickly as was polite, said goodbye and left. On the pavement outside the pub Tansey hesitated. It seemed ungrateful to leave Greenway there, but his hand was hurting and he was eager to get home.

The decision was made for him. 'I'll drive you, sir, if you'll show me where you live. Or does your hand need professional attention?'

'It may need it, but it's not going to get it—not tonight, anyway,' Tansey said. 'A hospital casualty department on a Sunday evening is not my idea of fun. You don't have a car?'

'No. I came with the others.'

Tansey didn't press the point. He explained the route to his home and let the sergeant drive. Although it was his own car he was used to being chauffeured by her, and the situation didn't seem in the least odd.

When they reached his house, Hilary Greenway said a little tentatively, 'If—if you've got any sort of first-aid kit, sir, I could do your hand. It'll be difficult for you.'

She expected him to refuse, but he didn't and by the time the hand was cleaned and expertly dressed they were both relaxed. And Tansey felt he owed her.

He said, 'There's a pheasant casserole in the fridge. If you'd put it in the oven we could have supper together—unless of course you've got other commitments.'

'I haven't, and I'm very fond of pheasant,' she said.

The evening passed pleasantly, though inevitably they talked shop. He recounted what Minden had told him, but a curious sense of embarrassment prevented him from producing the centre spread for Greenway's inspection. The sergeant left soon after supper. He insisted she take his car.

'I'm not having my sergeant walking about in the dark and disappearing,' he said. 'Just drive home in it, and pick me up at 8.00 a.m. tomorrow.'

CHAPTER 9

It took Sergeant Greenway very little time to discover where *Beautiful Butterflies* was printed and published—a small printing firm by the name of Ewan & Son in Reading which, in addition to a sideline in soft and hard-core pornography, also printed religious tracts, children's colouring books, and greetings cards of various kinds. The somewhat cynical Vice Squad officers who produced this information had taken no action against the business, largely because they held the view that to close down one particularly discreet firm was merely to encourage two or three others—probably less discreet—to open. Better the evil we know, they said.

In fact, Cyril Ewan and his son, Tom, gave every appearance of being respectable citizens. They attended their brand of chapel every Sunday. They did not smoke or drink or over-indulge themselves in any way. They gave to charitable appeals when requested, although this last virtue hurt them most because, if they had a vice, it was an excessive love of money.

It was this greed which, after a couple of bad years, had

driven them into the pornography industry, and they had
been innocently surprised to discover how paying porn could
be. To start with they had printed work—no questions
asked—for others to publish, but eventually, showing the
enterprise requested of all small businessmen, they had
branched out on their own with a magazine with a strictly
'controlled' circulation. *Beautiful Butterflies* was its title. The
periodical had proved a money-spinner, and the firm was
now on a very sound financial footing.

But even the Ewans were not so innocent as to be unaware
that, however carefully they conducted this aspect of their
trade, there could eventually be trouble with the police. The
trouble came in the form of Chief Inspector Tansey who,
accompanied by Sergeant Greenway, arrived at their plant
late on the Monday morning after Linda Jackson had disappeared.

Tom Ewan greeted them in an outer office, but as soon
as Tansey produced his warrant card and introduced himself
and Greenway, he at once showed them into a room where
Cyril Ewan was studying a book of samples of get-well
cards.

'And what can I do for you, Chief Inspector?' the older
Ewan asked. 'A contribution to the police sports fund,
perhaps?'

Cyril was in his mid-sixties. He had white hair and a
round cherubic face. When he smiled, as he did now, he
looked like everyone's idea of a benevolent grandfather. For
a moment Tansey wondered if they had been misinformed
by their colleagues, and had come to the wrong place
to interview the wrong characters. Cyril exuded virtuous
innocence.

There was nothing to do but go ahead, thought Tansey.
So: 'Mr Ewan,' he said, 'we have reason to believe you
publish a magazine called *Beautiful Butterflies*, which speci-
alizes in pictures of female nudes. Is that correct?'

Cyril didn't blanch or hesitate. 'Of course, Chief Inspector,' he said at once, 'that's correct. It's not the kind of magazine I would choose to read, and I very much doubt if you would either, but it's what many of the public seem to want these days. And if a man's to stay in business, he's got to move with the times and satisfy the current market.'

'No doubt,' Tansey said, somewhat taken aback at this businesslike reaction. He decided to get to the heart of the matter immediately. 'Mr Ewan,' he demanded brusquely, 'have you ever heard of Kate Minden?'

'No—o. I don't think—'

'She's one of the Oxfordshire young ladies who disappeared, Pa,' Tom Ewan said.

Cyril's smile faded, and he frowned. 'But what is she to do with us?' he asked, apparently bewildered.

Slowly Tansey took the centre spread from his inside breast pocket and opened it on the desk in front of Cyril Ewan. Sergeant Greenway had already seen the pictures; Tansey had found it easier to show them to her in the formal atmosphere of the office that morning than in the course of what had turned out to be a pleasant and casual evening together the night before. He had sensed her instinctive disgust, overlaid by professional interest. Neither of the Ewans showed any emotion.

'That's the missing girl?' Tom said disbelievingly.

'Yes! And I want to know where you got these photographs.' The Chief Inspector changed his tack and became authoritative. He turned and gave Tom a cold stare. Tom, who was a younger version of his father, stared back. 'Believe me,' Tansey went on, 'I'm not interested in charging either of you with publishing or distributing pornography. If any charge is made it will probably be of abduction—possibly leading to murder, if Miss Minden is not found alive. So in your own interests you'd better understand that this is a serious matter.'

There was a long silence. The two Ewans stared at each other in surprise. It seemed that neither of them had been

prepared for even a suggestion of any such accusation. With
luck, even if they were to be accused and found guilty of
publishing pornography, they might expect only a heavy
fine. Abduction, not to mention murder, was in quite a
different class.

Cyril said, 'Chief Inspector, we'll tell you whatever we
can. Unfortunately, I doubt if it'll be as much as you may
hope. These photographs—you say they're of Kate Minden
—were sent to us by a fairly regular contributor to *Butterflies*.
We know him as J. P. Browne—spelt with an "e"— but
that's all we do know about him. And I doubt if that's his
usual name.'

'You've got an address? You can describe him?' demanded Tansey eagerly.

Cyril Ewan shook his head. 'Tom, you explain.'

Tom said, 'Browne started sending us batches of colour
transparencies—' He paused and glanced at the police
officers. Then, 'That's what the trade calls artwork like 35
mm colour slides,' he explained. 'Anyway, he sent these
pictures through the mail about five months ago. They were
unsolicited, but that's often the case with pix of this kind.
Technically they were extremely good, but they weren't
really suitable for *Butterflies*' readership.' He made it sound
as if he were discussing a literary magazine. 'They relied
too much on artefacts—props, if you like.'

Here Tom Ewan threw an anxious look at Sergeant
Greenway, as if he didn't approve of her presence at such a
discussion. 'And—and only parts of the—er—the anatomy
were shown. We suspected blow-ups from other publications. Anyway, we returned them, but we told Browne we
might be interested if he could give us full figures. And
about three weeks ago he came up with a collection of pix
of that red-head. They were so brilliant we scrapped the
centre spread we'd planned, and gave it over to her completely. But I assure you we'd no reason to think it might
be Kate Minden. You can't see her face in any of them.'

'I appreciate that,' said Tansey. 'But she's been identified, nevertheless, and we need to talk to Browne. You mentioned returning photos to him, and you've got to pay him somehow.'

'So far we've only paid him a couple of times.' Cyril took up the story. 'He asked for cash. Again, that's not unusual among our contributors. And we sent it to a shop in Oxford, which we expect is an accommodation address. Naturally, we'll give it to you, Chief Inspector, for what good it'll do.'

'It might help a great deal,' Tansey said sharply. 'Now, we shall expect you to continue publishing Browne's pictures until we tell you to stop, and you must keep us informed of any further developments. You understand? *Quid pro quo*. We'll think of you as part of our team for the moment. Don't forget the other two girls, either. Long hair, remember.'

Father and son nodded in unison. They knew precisely what the Chief Inspector meant. No prosecution. No folding of the profitable *Butterflies*, at least for a while. No scandal. No disgrace for themselves or their families. No gossip among friends or neighbours. It was an excellent bargain from their point of view.

Cyril nodded at Tom, and Tom said, 'Chief Inspector, we were going to tell you, and I've got a suggestion that might help your inquiries. We *have* received some more pix from this Browne. Two lots. We've paid for the first, but the second only arrived today. If we post the money right away, it'll arrive tomorrow or the next day. Would that give you time to have a word with the owner of the shop, and perhaps stake it out, as you call it?'

'Yes, it would.' Tansey was not surprised at this eager cooperation; it was no more than he had expected. But the photographs that were not yet paid for represented a bonus. 'We must see these two lots you haven't published yet— and any other future contributions.'

'Of course,' said Tom. 'I'll fetch them.'

'Are they all of Kate Minden?' Tansey asked Cyril as Tom left the office.

'No. There's another—' Cyril's innocent blue eyes widened in horror. 'Chief Inspector, are you thinking what I'm thinking?'

'What would that be, Mr Ewan?'

'According to the papers there's been a spate of missing girls, but there was no reason, no reason at all, why we should have associated them with Browne's models. Girls who pose for that kind of picture must do it mainly for the money, though some, I believe, get a kick out of it, but— Oh, this is dreadful, dreadful—'

Cyril Ewan might have been a hypocrite in some ways, but now he gave every appearance of being genuinely upset. He was still shaking his head when his son returned with a couple of envelopes in one hand, and a small light-box under the other arm. He handed the envelopes to the Chief Inspector and plugged in the box. Tansey took the transparencies from the first envelope and scattered them over the ground glass screen, handling them carefully by the edges of their cardboard mounts, as Tom Ewan had done. He thought of fingerprints, but decided there would be little hope; Browne was too careful. However, they must go through the motions, and get specimen prints from the Ewans and anyone else in the printing works who might have touched them.

As in the centre spread of the issue of *Beautiful Butterflies* they had seen, these transparencies depicted Kate Minden, but here she was posed with a second girl, a long-haired brunette. The poses were equally disgusting and, if anything, more erotic.

'Let me see, sir.'

There was a muffled protest from the Ewans, but Tansey drew back, knowing that it was inevitable that his sergeant should view the evidence. He emptied the second envelope on to the lighted glass. More of the brunette, he thought, with her long hair still hiding her face. Thoughtfully, he heaped the transparencies into a neat pile, and waited.

'I'd say there's very little doubt, sir,' Sergeant Greenway remarked matter-of-factly.

Tansey nodded. 'We'll have to take all these—'

Tom Ewan interrupted him. 'If you do that how can we print them, as you wanted?' he demanded.

'Yes, I see,' said Tansey. 'Well, I'll make sure copies are returned to you in a couple of days, Mr Ewan—'

'Not copies,' Tom Ewan interrupted him again. 'Browne hasn't asked for his transparencies back, but he could do so. We'd have to send him originals.'

'All right,' Tansey conceded. 'You'll get the originals back in a day or two. We'll give you a receipt, of course.'

He paused a moment, then added, 'And I've got a suspicion you may get a further batch, or two or three, quite soon. If so, as I said, let us know at once, and handle them with great care. Remember the chance of fingerprints. And give us that accommodation address. Go ahead and pay Browne as if we'd never visited you this morning. Then with luck we'll get him, and maybe find these wretched girls alive.'

'Please God, yes, let us hope so,' Cyril said piously and Tom, following his father's lead, bowed his head as if in silent prayer.

'Minden and Rust without a doubt, as you said, Sergeant,' Tansey commented on their way back to Oxford. 'But no Jackson—'

'There's hardly been time, sir,' Greenway protested. 'She only went missing on Friday night, and it must take a little while to—to persuade—'

'I know, I know,' said Tansey wearily. 'This case is getting me down. I expect the Jackson girl will be in the next batch, if we don't get to Browne, or whoever, first.'

They had no difficulty in finding Hunter's at the address

the Ewans had given them. It was a newsagent's in a mean, narrow street not far from Oxford railway station, and was similar to many other struggling little stores all over the country. As well as papers it sold cigarettes, sweets, paperback books, stationery, film and a variety of similar goods. Its window and glass-fronted showcases beside the door were almost obliterated by small advertisements. These offered for sale every imaginable article from a used wedding dress to a suite of furniture, invited attractive middle-aged gentlemen to meet similar ladies and, among other less euphemistically-worded diversions, promised relief from all bodily pains and tensions with sessions of massage and physiotherapy. A bell over the door rang loudly as the two detectives went into the shop.

'Mr Hunter?' Tansey addressed the man behind the crowded counter.

'Yes. I'm Gus Hunter. So what?'

He was a small man with a narrow face, and his sad eyes, set too close together, reminded Greenway of a fox. But he showed no dismay when Tansey identified himself and his sergeant. He gave the impression that this was not the first time he'd been visited by the police.

'Browne. Browne with an "e",' he said. 'J. P. Browne. Yes, I seem to remember a couple of thick envelopes.' He opened a drawer in the counter and shuffled around in it. 'There's nothing here for J. P. Browne at the moment. They must have been collected.'

Tansey had expected this; it was unlikely that Browne would leave any correspondence waiting at the accommodation address for very long. He paused impatiently while a man bought cigarettes, and a small boy chose between chocolate bars. Then he returned to the attack.

'Don't you keep any records?' he demanded roughly.

'Records? Records of these individual letters? No. Why should I? I keep accounts, of course. How much they pay me, and so on. But I charge a standard fee for this accommodation address service, so all I've got is the name and the date of each payment.'

'I see. Very sensible, I'm sure,' said Tansey sardonically. 'Well, just describe Browne for us.'

Hunter thought for a moment. 'Tall. I couldn't say what colour his hair is. He wore a tweed hat. Pleasant enough manner. Takes what's there for him and goes.' Hunter paused. 'No particular accent. Talks more or less posh. A gent, but not one born to it, if you know what I mean.'

'Moustache? Limp? Anything to distinguish him?' said Tansey. 'What other clothes did he wear, apart from his hat?'

'A raincoat and slacks, I think. He looked like any other guy. Youngish to middle-aged, I'd guess.'

'But you'd know him again?'

There was the slightest hesitation before Hunter said, 'Sure, I'd recognize him again.' His mouth twitched as if he were smothering a yawn, or a grin at some private joke.

'How did he come here? In a car, on foot, or a motorcycle?' Tansey persisted.

'On foot, as far as I know, but he could have had transport parked around the corner, couldn't he?' Hunter had begun to sound bored. 'Look, I wasn't all that interested in him. Why should I be? I provide a service to the public, as I've told you—an address for private correspondence. There's nothing illegal about it. It's a service that's needed. You'd be surprised—'

Tansey cut him short. 'Okay, Mr Hunter. Now, listen. A thick letter will be arriving in the next day or so for Mr J. P. Browne with an "e". When he comes to collect it— which he will quite soon—you don't do anything. Just hand it over as usual. I assume that door there leads to your own premises?' Hunter nodded, and Tansey continued. 'Fine. Well, there'll be a plain-clothes officer behind it. Just give him a signal and leave the rest to us. You understand? Later perhaps you'll be asked to be a witness.'

'Yes. But I can't afford to be away from my business for long,' said Hunter weakly.

'The price of being a good citizen,' Tansey said with false sympathy and, as a couple of women came into the shop, gestured to Greenway that it was time to go.

'You're not happy about the situation, are you, sir?' Sergeant Greenway said tentatively as she drove them back to Headquarters.

'Not wildly,' Tansey admitted. 'For one thing I don't trust Hunter. He never asked why we were so keen to interview Browne, which would have been a natural reaction. And it could have been a mistake, but he was wrong about Browne's letters. He suggested there had been only one or two, whereas the Ewans say they sent back the pictures that were no use to them. So three or four would have been more accurate. And there was something odd about Hunter's manner. I'm pretty sure he knows more about Browne than he told us.'

'His description certainly wasn't much use, but I suppose he can't be expected to know all his customers.'

'Maybe not those who occasionally buy cigarettes or sweets, but I'd be surprised if he doesn't take an interest in those who use his address.' Tansey shrugged. 'Of course, it's possible he just dislikes the police, and has no inclination to help us. Maybe we should have checked him out before we called on him. Do it as soon as we get back, will you, Sergeant?'

'Yes, sir.' Greenway drove smoothly into a parking space beside the long, low Headquarters building. 'You know, sir, I'm sorry, but I still do not understand how Kate Minden and presumably Linda Jackson—let's forget young Mary —two sensible girls, could have gone with this man, Browne or whatever his name is, in the first place. And I can't conceive why they should allow themselves to be photographed in those revolting poses. They can't have been hypnotized, can they?'

'I don't know,' said Tansey, 'but I doubt it. I imagine Browne has a chum. One of them takes the photographs, and the other stands by and keeps guard, as it were. Earlier you mentioned persuasion, my dear sergeant. Well, a gun or a knife can be powerful persuaders.'

CHAPTER 10

'I'm sorry, ladies and gentlemen. There's no more I can tell you at present.'

Chief Inspector Tansey pushed his way through the reporters, ignoring the cameras that searched his face, and found refuge inside his Headquarters. He marched along the bare corridors to his office, wondering why there was such a renewed outburst of media interest in the case. It was now Tuesday, and the news of Linda Jackson's disappearance had been fully covered in the Sundays, naturally with a variety of more or less sensational references to Kate Minden and Mary Rust.

He found Sergeant Greenway in his office, sitting at his desk and speaking into the telephone. She made to rise as he came in but he motioned to her to stay where she was. She finished the conversation quickly.

'Sorry, sir, but since that nine o'clock newscast last night we've been inundated with calls. Mostly from the families, but that one was actually from Mr Quayle, Brian's father.'

Tansey sat down in the chair she had vacated. 'Sergeant,' he said. 'I don't know what you're talking about. I haven't heard any news. My sister and brother-in-law were in Oxford yesterday evening visiting their son, who's just come up to the university, and we had a family dinner. As a result I overslept this morning, which is why I'm late.'

'I—I see.' Greenway hadn't been prepared for a personal explanation. 'Well, sir, it seems that some joker rang the TV people late yesterday afternoon, and said that the police had made a breakthrough, and Detective Chief Inspector Tansey was confident that the abductor of the three missing girls would be arrested in the next day or so.'

Tansey drew a deep breath and expelled it through his teeth. Useless to ask if anyone had checked with the Kidlington press office, or who or why someone had leaked a comment to the media, he realized. The damage was done. Browne could hardly fail to be on his guard. If he were clever he'd lie low for a while, get rid of the girls—bury them in his basement, perhaps. And if he were determined he'd probably eventually start up again with a brand new collection of butterflies.

He controlled his temper and his imagination. 'We'll continue the Hunter operation as planned,' he said at last. 'It's all we can do. The men should be on their way to the shop by now.'

'Yes. They've already left, sir.'

'Good. If Browne doesn't turn up to collect his money by next week at the latest, we'll know he's been scared off and we can forget Hunter as a lead. Anything else, Sergeant?'

'Yes, sir. About Hunter. You told me to check on him. He's never been inside, but about a couple of years ago he was charged with attempted blackmail and, I gather, was lucky to get off.'

'Blackmail? Mm—m, I'm not surprised. His accommodation address business could lend itself to that sort of thing.'

The telephone rang, 'What?' Tansey said loudly. He signalled to Greenway to stay. 'I'll be right along, as soon as I've arranged for a scene of crime team and a police surgeon. There's a surgeon on the way? Fine. Meanwhile, you know enough not to touch a thing. Put a man on the door to turn customers away. But make sure he takes in any mail. And get someone to go round the neighbours to ask if they heard or saw anything.'

The Chief Inspector snapped the receiver back into place. 'Browne's managed to keep a step ahead of us, I'd say,' he remarked. 'At any rate, Hunter's dead. Someone called on him last night—he lived alone behind and over his shop—and strangled him.'

Gus Hunter was not a pretty sight. He lay on his back on the floor of the small room behind the shop, which had clearly served him as a living-room. His face was blotched. His eyes stared from their sockets. His tongue, which he had bitten badly, protruded obscenely between his teeth. There was also a hideous wound over his right ear, on which blood had clotted.

'In my opinion, he was struck from behind, probably as he was showing a visitor into the room,' the police surgeon said. 'To judge from the wound the proverbial blunt instrument could have been something like a large spanner. The blow didn't kill him, but he'd have been stunned, and after that it was easy to strangle the man. He was small and slight, as you see. But the pathologist will be able to tell you more after the PM.'

'Thanks,' the Chief Inspector said, grateful that this police surgeon had been so forthcoming; so often these doctors were unprepared to commit themselves at an early stage, in case the later full pathologist's report proved them wrong. Tansey decided he might as well press his luck. 'Any idea of the time?' he asked casually.

The doctor considered. 'Between eleven last night and two this morning, if you want a guess. But again, we can be more accurate when we've had a look at his innards. Let us know if you get any idea what he had to eat or drink, won't you?'

'Of course.' Tansey thanked him again, and the police surgeon, having packed his bag, hurried away. Tansey turned to the inspector who was in charge of the scene of crime team, and waited for his report.

'No sign of a break-in, sir. It must have been someone Hunter knew, or was expecting.' The Inspector pointed to a bottle of whisky on the table, three-quarters full, with two glasses. 'He'd had a drink before his chum arrived. The prints on the glass that was used are his. The other was unused, though it also has a few of his prints, presumably from getting it out of the cupboard. Anyway, the main thing is that the killer didn't waste any time drinking with him first.'

Sergeant Greenway came into the back room from the shop. 'Sir, I've a lady—a Mrs Sandra Lloyd—whom I think you should speak to. She may have seen Hunter's visitor.'

Sandra Lloyd was an attractive young woman in her late twenties, and Tansey was glad to see that she looked intelligent and sensible. He shook hands with her, and brought a chair from behind the counter for her to sit on, but she ignored it.

'I can't stop. I've left my little girl with her dad, but he works nights and wants to go to bed.'

'All right, Mrs Lloyd, we'll be as quick as we can. Just tell us what you saw and when,' Tansey said.

'It was about eleven-thirty last night. Maureen, my little girl, was restless, and at last I'd just got her off to sleep. I don't know why, but I went to the window. We live across the street, and Maureen's room's in the front, so I could see Hunter's shop doorway. It was open, and someone came out. But it was dark, of course, and the street lights around here don't help much. I couldn't tell you what he looked like. I'm sorry.'

'It was a man, though,' said Tansey at once.

'It wore trousers, at least,' said Mrs Lloyd.

'Fine. You've been a big help, Mrs Lloyd. Assuming that this was the individual who attacked Mr Hunter, we've now got a time. That could be vital. We're very grateful.' He smiled at her. 'Can you recall anything else?'

'Not really. It was just a tallish shadow.' Mrs Lloyd screwed up her face in an effort to remember the scene. 'I've a vague impression of a limp, but I'm not sure about that. I did hear a car, though, two or three minutes after he'd gone. Of course, it could have had nothing to do with him, but it might have, mightn't it? He wouldn't have wanted to park right outside, would he?'

'I shouldn't think so. Not if he's the person in question,' Tansey assured her. 'But we'll make inquiries.' With renewed thanks he showed her to the door, and turned to face Greenway. 'A limp?' he said.

'Only a vague impression,' the sergeant corrected him.

'Point taken,' Tansey conceded. 'But at least we're certain of one thing. Whoever killed Hunter was not Kate Minden's husband, as we've still got him safely in the cells—I must deal with him as soon as we get back to Headquarters,' the Chief Inspector added parenthetically. 'In the meantime it would be interesting to find out which of the people involved in the case have anything approaching an alibi for last night.'

'You're assuming that it was Browne who murdered Hunter, sir?'

'Let's say it's a very tempting scenario. We know that Hunter's got—had—a dicey background as a blackmailer. Let's suppose he got interested in this particular client of his. Suppose he steamed open the first thick packet—the one containing the slides the Ewans returned. So—an opportunity? What do you suppose Hunter might think—that he could be on to a good thing? Especially if he discovered that later envelopes contained cash.'

'Why didn't he try to blackmail Browne over the slides the Ewans returned?'

'Because Browne would probably have told him to go to hell. After all, he'd done nothing criminal then—except

possibly sending obscene materials through the mail—and
what's that likely to amount to?'

'It could amount to a good deal, sir, depending on our
Browne's position, if he were charged with a crime like that.'

'Possibly. But his situation's much worse once he's sent
off the pictures of the missing girls. And if he learns he's
wanted by the police—and after we interviewed Hunter it
was clear we wanted Browne badly—the whole affair's on
a different level.'

'I see your point, sir. As soon as we'd left Hunter phones
Browne—he must have discovered who Browne really was.
Hunter tells him about us and our plans, and promises to
spill the beans if Browne doesn't produce. Browne promises
to bring him money, or meet him to arrange to deal him in,
or something, and instead . . . I wonder, sir, could it have
been Hunter who phoned that TV station to say we were
about to make an arrest? It might have convinced Browne
he wasn't lying.'

Tansey nodded. 'I hadn't thought of that,' he admitted
with a wry grin. 'But if Hunter was a blackmailer he must
have had other victims. We mustn't be tempted too much,
Sergeant. His death may be nothing to do with Browne.
You and I were always taught not to jump at the obvious.
On the other hand, I've learnt over the years that the
obvious often turns out to be correct. Let's keep an open
mind for the moment, shall we?'

'As you say, sir,' said Greenway. 'But whether Browne
was the killer, or Hunter's death was just a ridiculous
coincidence, I'm afraid we've lost the Hunter–Browne connection as a lead to those girls.'

Someone once remarked that a successful police investigation depended on ninety-nine per cent dogged routine
work, and one per cent inspiration. Tansey would have
agreed with this dictum.

During the rest of that week many individuals were interviewed, alibis were checked, the phone rang constantly, reports were filed. Only the inspiration was lacking. By Friday evening Tansey had made no progress with his inquiry, though he and his colleagues had amassed a considerable number of conceivably relevant facts.

They had learnt, for example, that a Ford Escort—colour blue or green—had been parked two streets away from Hunter's shop on the night of the murder, and had been seen to drive away at about 11.30 p.m. The fact that Hunter was a small-time blackmailer had been confirmed; a man had been traced who, under pressure, had admitted that he had used the accommodation address to correspond with his mistress, and that Hunter had taken advantage of this situation. On the night of Hunter's death, however, he had been out of the country.

Others involved had less satisfactory alibis, or none at all. Peter Cousin, who had not been at work on Monday, claimed to have been nursing a cold in his Cotswold cottage. Brian Quayle said that he had been on a pub crawl round Oxford with some friends, but none of them could confirm that he had been with them all the time; what was more, they had all come to Oxford in Brian's father's car, and Brian's father, like thousands of others, drove a blue Ford Escort.

Of the rest of those involved, Dr Paul Avery had been on duty at the Radcliffe Infirmary, but might not have been missed if he had absented himself for half an hour. Cyril Ewan and son Tom maintained that they were at home, watching television. Quentin Wood told the police officers who called on him that it was no damned business of theirs where he'd been on Monday night, and would they please stop bothering him. None of this was particularly helpful.

Meanwhile, Steve Minden had appeared in court, charged with a number of offences, including assaulting police officers; the magistrates had taken a serious view of the matter and remanded him in custody for a week. This could be seen—and was seen by the media—as the only definitive step taken by the police since the last disappearance, in spite of the rumoured breakthrough.

'We're not getting anywhere fast,' Tansey said despondently on the Friday afternoon. 'Browne was such a great lead, but now we're back where we started. It's quite possible that so far we've never even come across Browne; there's no reason why he should have any direct connection with any of the missing girls. For all we know he's just a brilliant photographer who likes taking pornographic pictures, and he picked on these girls because of their looks and their figures—as you once implied, Sergeant.' He smiled sadly. 'And here we are, at another weekend.'

'You're afraid—' Greenway began.

'Yes. Aren't you? Our joker always seems to strike at weekends.'

'That could be chance, sir. If he's spotted a girl and followed her around, he may just seize an opportunity when it arises.'

'True, Sergeant. All the same, I'll be thankful to reach Monday without another disappearance.'

'He can't go on collecting girls indefinitely, sir. There are questions of space, facilities, shopping, feeding them—all sorts of practical points. Their hair will need attention, for one thing. He seems keen on beautiful long hair.'

Tansey nodded his agreement, his thoughts elsewhere. There was something about the pictures in that centre spread from *Beautiful Butterflies* that had niggled at him ever since he had seen them, but he still couldn't define what was at the back of his mind. It had to concern Kate Minden, because she was the only girl featured in the spread, the only girl who had been abducted when those particular pictures were taken—but that was as far as he had got. There was no future in worrying at that bone, he reflected. The point would come to him sooner or later, or it wouldn't.

He looked at his watch. It was time to call it a day. He

said good night to Sergeant Greenway with a brusqueness he
didn't intend. Their relationship had changed imperceptibly
since the previous Sunday when she had driven him home
after Steve Minden's attack in the Black Boar, bandaged
his hand and stayed to supper. But he was too tired to face
the implications of this fact, and he was glad when she had
gone, and he was alone.

CHAPTER 11

As far as Chief Inspector Tansey was concerned the weekend
passed without incident. He remained in touch with Headquarters by phone, and learnt that no one in the area served
by the Thames Valley Police was reported missing; there
were of course a number of missing persons elsewhere in the
country, but none seemed as if they could be even remotely
related to his problems.

He had just arrived at his office early on Monday morning
when disaster struck. There was a knock at the door and
Sergeant Greenway appeared. He looked up hopefully;
usually she produced a cup of coffee. But one glance at the
Sergeant's face was enough to tell him that she was bringing
bad news.

'Sir, a report has just come in. A man—apparently a
middle-aged don called Basil Donnelly—was walking his
dog in Parks half an hour ago when the dog became interested in something caught in the bushes at the side of the
River Cherwell. The dog persisted, and wouldn't come when
called, so Mr Donnelly climbed down the bank to see
and—'

Tansey put his elbows on his desk and rested his chin
between his hands. 'Which one is it?' he demanded harshly.
'Or is it a fourth?'

'I don't know, sir. It could be none of them. The body's

certainly that of a young woman, but it had been in the water some time, and the face was . . . there was no face.'

'No face? What the hell do you mean?'

'Acid, they guess, sir.'

'What about hair? That's an obvious pointer.'

'She had none, sir. Her whole body had been shaved.'

'Good God!' Tansey sighed. 'Well, we don't need actual hair to know what colour it would be, and we don't necessarily need a face, especially if the teeth are intact. And the fact that our friend got rid of her hair suggests the field's pretty limited. He's merely delayed identification slightly. What about her clothes?'

'She was naked.'

'As one might have expected. Right. Let's get down there.' Tansey was on his feet. 'Then I'll want to see this Mr Donnelly.'

'Mr Donnelly reported his find to St Aldate's station, sir, and they acted at once. The police surgeon and the scene of crime boys are already on the spot, and the pathologist is on his way, they say.'

'Fine. Let's go and join them,' said the Chief Inspector.

They drove to the edge of Parks, where a police van and several cars were standing. The uniformed officer on duty with them hastily extinguished his cigarette as the Chief Inspector arrived. He came forward and saluted.

'Good morning, sir. The inspector said I was to expect you. He's down by the river about there, sir, superintending the search of the area. The surgeon's there, too, and the pathologist.'

'Thanks. We'll join them.'

They greeted the police surgeon and the pathologist beside a sheet-covered figure lying on the grass by the river bank. They had obviously completed their preliminary examination.

The pathologist said gloomily, 'Well, there you are, Chief

Inspector. There's not much we can tell you. In the water for a while. Cause of death unknown until the PM. Time of death uncertain, for the moment. The sooner we get her moved the better. I suppose you must see her.'

'It's not a pretty sight,' said the pathologist, glancing at Greenway.

'We were told about the face,' said Tansey.

The surgeon pulled down the sheet, and both Tansey and Greenway drew sharp breaths.

'One of the worst I've seen in years,' said the pathologist. 'Acid. At a guess, fuming nitric.'

'Is that used in photography?' asked Tansey sharply.

'I don't think so,' said the surgeon. 'Hydrochloric used to be used as a photographic toning agent, I believe. But we'll check, naturally.'

At this point the scene of crime inspector who had been supervising the search of the river bank both upstream and downstream made his apearance. 'Good morning, sir,' he said. 'The photography's complete and the mortuary van just arrived.'

'Great,' said the pathologist. 'Look, Chief Inspector. Let's get her out of here, and see if we can find out any more.'

'All right,' said Tansey. 'But just one thing. I want to see her buttocks.'

'Buttocks?' said the pathologist in surprise.

'Yes.'

'Well—' Together they rolled the body over, and there on the right cheek was the strawberry mark. 'Make sure you get a photo of that, Inspector. In colour, too—and right here on the site. We can take another during the PM. It won't fade after death, will it?' he asked, turning to the doctors.

'No, no,' said the pathologist. 'There's no question of it disappearing. But why—'

Tansey had just time to say, 'I'll tell you later,' before there was a choking sound behind them, and he managed to turn and catch Sergeant Greenway as she fell. He laid her carefully on the ground, and the police surgeon started towards her.

But the sergeant was already regaining consciousness. 'I —I'm sorry. I'm so sorry. It was all too much. The face— the shaving—the mark. But to faint! I've seen bodies before, but I've never done that. I—I really am sorry, sir.'

'It's all right. When I saw my first mutilated corpse I vomited all over the floor of the mortuary. That was much worse,' said Tansey, squatting down beside her.

'Really? You're not saying that—'

The pathologist and the police surgeon had been eyeing their watches, and the surgeon intervened. 'If you're all right, Sergeant, we've got to leave. I suggest the usual remedy for shock—hot, sweet tea, when you can get some.' Then to Tansey. 'You'll attend the PM, I imagine.'

'Yes,' Tansey said, 'and thank you so much, both of you. That mark—it's vital. It identifies the body as Kate Minden. It'll have to be confirmed but I don't think there's much doubt. And I've got her husband who'll make a formal identification.'

'Good,' said the surgeon. 'I noticed it earlier, and wondered if it might help.'

'We'll get out of here ourselves as soon as we can,' Tansey said to Hilary Greenway when the two doctors had left. 'Are you feeling better?'

She nodded. 'Poor Kate!' she said. 'I—I'd so much hoped it wouldn't be Kate. She's had such a ghastly life with that husband of hers, and there's the little girl, Zelda.'

'Zelda has a loving grandmother who'll take care of her,' Tansey said firmly, 'and Kate's beyond suffering. What we have to do is find her killer. That's our job, Sergeant, and we should get on with it as soon as possible.'

For a second Hilary Greenway thought the Chief Inspector was being unpleasant. Then she realized that his smile was full of sympathy, and that he was holding her hand tightly. His words had been intended to help her pull herself together. She sniffed, nodded and returned his smile.

'I—I'm all right now, Thank you—sir,' she said.

'Okay.' Tansey rose and pulled Greenway to her feet. 'If you're sure you're okay, just let us have another word with the inspector, and we'll be on our way.'

The inspector's team were spread out in a line, combing the bank for possible clues. It was slow, tedious work, and so far had yielded no result.

'This is where the dog found the body, sir. It got caught up in the roots there, but it could have been put into the river a half-mile or more upstream, depending on the timing. The current's sluggish on this stretch but, given time, anything will drift down providing it doesn't get entangled in the weeds.'

'Is there much hope of finding just where she was put in?'

'Not much, sir.' The inspector shook his head. 'As you see, I've got men searching the banks for any signs, but it's a forlorn hope.' He turned and eyed Greenway appraisingly. 'She was somewhat the same build as the Sergeant here. Not heavy. But I doubt if anyone would want to carry her for very long. So possibly she was put in fairly close to a road.'

'Possibly,' said Tansey, carefully keeping any suggestion of amusement from his voice as he saw Greenway's head come up sharply at the mention of her weight. 'However slight, she wouldn't have been an easy burden, quite apart from the chance of being seen.'

'And as well as the current, there's also the question of weather, sir. It rained very heavily around three this morning, so if she was put in the water before that any evidence the killer may have left has probably been washed away.'

'Hmm. Well, keep at it, Inspector. We've not had much luck with this case up to now,' Tansey said, 'so perhaps we're due for some. Sergeant, I think we'll go and get some tea, before we talk with this Mr Donnelly.'

*

Though he was willing enough, Bernard Donnelly proved of little assistance. He was a small, thin man in his late forties, who looked as if a good gust of wind would blow him from Oxfordshire into the next county. He lived with his wife and three children, coincidentally in the same crescent as Quentin Wood, and he was a Fellow of the same college.

'It never occurred to me that—that what I found, or rather what Rufus found—was one of those missing girls, not until I saw Quentin drive off in his Jaguar as the police were kindly delivering me home here; he reminded me of Linda Jackson, naturally. Stupid of me, I know—not to think of it earlier, I mean—but it was all something of a shock, as I'm sure you'll appreciate. Middle-aged dons aren't accustomed to happening on bodies while they're taking their dogs for early-morning walks.'

'No, of course not,' Tansey agreed. 'And we're grateful to you for being so cooperative.'

'More than old Quentin's been, I gather.' Donnelly chortled; that was the only word to describe his laugh. 'He's really cut up about Linda Jackson. She was one of his brightest pupils, and he was fond of her, even though she refused to let him take photographs of her—'

'Photographs?' interrupted Tansey.

'Oh yes. Quentin's brilliant with his camera. He's even had exhibitions. Local galleries, certainly. But good, nevertheless. I do hope it wasn't Linda Jackson whose body Rufus found.'

'The body hasn't been identified yet,' said Tansey carefully. He knew it was a half-lie, for there was no doubt in his mind that it was Kate who had been killed, and that her husband would make a positive identification.

'Why do you think Linda Jackson should mind being photographed?' Greenway asked innocently.

Donnelly shrugged. 'Silly of her, I expect, but Quentin

has something of a reputation, in spite of being a grandpa now, and I dare say she thought that posing for him might encourage him to make a pass at her.'

'But perhaps he just wanted to take her portrait. After all, she's a beautiful girl.'

'Perhaps,' said Donnelly, though he didn't sound as if he believed this. 'Quentin's certainly a keen photographer. He's got a darkroom in his basement, and all kinds of equipment.'

At that point the telephone rang, and Tansey said they would see themselves out. The Chief Inspector was addicted to concluding interviews inconclusively, Hilary Greenway reflected, but perhaps his technique paid off in the end.

The Chief Inspector was thoughtful as he got into the car, but Greenway couldn't contain herself.

'What an unpleasant little man,' she said.

'But interesting, Sergeant. And, remember, they're members of the same college, and we don't know anything about college politics or in-fighting.'

'No, we don't,' said Sergeant Greenway a little doubtfully. Then, 'Do you want to go straight to Wood's house now, sir?'

'No. Back to HQ, please. We know that Wood's out, and his housekeeper wouldn't let us see around without his permission. I doubt if he himself would, unless we had a search warrant. And incidentally, the fact that he's got a housekeeper hardly suggests that he's keeping a harem of girls in his basement, does it? Even if she weren't allowed down there, she'd have to be pretty dumb not to realize that something was going on. And Wood drives a Jaguar, though I guess he could have an Escort stashed away somewhere too.'

Tansey was thinking aloud again. 'It's one step forward and two steps back all the time,' he said bitterly. Then he lapsed into a silence, which lasted until they were nearing Kidlington. At this point he suddenly snapped his fingers.

'Got it! Something's been troubling me for days, and at last I've realized what it is.'

'Sir?'

'Sergeant, when we were interviewing Quentin Wood the other day, did you notice he had on his desk a photograph of a baby lying on its front with a bow round its middle?'

'Yes. It was a little kitchy, but a super picture, nevertheless. It might well have won a prize.'

'Now, I admit you didn't have a chance to examine those pages from *Beautiful Butterflies* in any detail—'

'No. You seemed to think they weren't suitable for me—sir. But what—'

'One of the reproductions—the one by which Minden recognized his wife because of the mark on her bottom—was very similar, except that, being an adult, it was indecent. It was much the same pose, and what made it particularly obscene was the huge bow of ribbon. It was as if the woman were offering herself like a box of chocolates—' Tansey stopped abruptly.

'I know exactly what you've got in mind,' said Greenway. 'It was as if she were for sale. Gift-wrapped.'

'Exactly.' Tansey heaved a sigh of relief at the lack of need for further explanation. 'Now, what's important is the timing. Kate was abducted on Friday evening, we assume. The Ewans received the photographs on, say, Tuesday. The magazine was printed and distributed the following Friday or Saturday—and that's including revamping the centre spread, if the Ewans are to be believed. So when did Wood take that shot of the baby? If it was after he had seen the magazine, we've nothing against him. But if it was before—'

'If it was before, he'd hardly have kept his inspiration on his desk, would he, sir? The baby's picture was on plain view when we were there. He'd obviously made no attempt to hide it. So the housekeeper should know when it appeared, unless . . . You've accepted that the abductor, the murderer, the man we know as Browne, had an accomplice. Could it

be that Quentin Wood and his housekeeper . . .' Greenway
let her sentence fade.

'It's conceivable,' said Tansey after a pause. 'If there had
been a woman in the car, both Kate and Mary would have
been more likely to accept a lift, and we've only Wood's
word that Linda ever left his house. Stranger couplings
than Wood and his housekeeper have been known, but . . .
Anyway, you'd better look into her, Sergeant.'

'Yes, sir. I—Damn!'

As Sergeant Greenway expertly swung the car into the
large parking lot beside Thames Valley Police Headquarters, a figure had practically thrown himself under her
wheels. Only by jamming on her brakes had she managed
not to hit him. As it was, he had slipped and fallen.

The Chief Inspector was out of the car, and helping him
to his feet. 'My dear Dr Avery, what on earth do you think
you're doing? Trying to commit suicide?'

Paul Avery seized Tansey by the arm. 'Miss Foyne told
me. She'd heard an item on her car radio as she was coming
back from the shops. One of the missing girls has been
pulled out of the Cherwell. Is it Linda? Is it my wife?'

'Yes, who is it, Chief Inspector?'

'Have you identified the body yet?'

'Is it true she had acid thrown at her face?'

There was a chorus of questions. As if from nowhere
a group of reporters had materialized. Cameras clicked.
Sergeant Greenway hooted angrily, edging the car forward
but, laughing, a cameraman seated himself on the bonnet
and photographed her through the windscreen.

'Naughty! Naughty!' he said as she swore at him.

'You're wasting your time and mine, gentlemen.' The
Chief Inspector was brusque. 'Any formal statement will
come from our press office, but I'm prepared to say that the
body found in the river has not yet been formally identified.
You can't expect me to make guesses. I expect there'll be a
press release, and perhaps a press conference this evening.

Now, if you'll let me—and my sergeant—pass, we'll get on with our work. Dr Avery, you get in the car.'

They grumbled, but quite good-naturedly, and let him go. Greenway drove on and parked in her accustomed slot. Tansey turned to Paul, who was biting his bottom lip and breathing deeply, but was once more in control of his emotions.

'Come on in, Doctor. I want to talk to you anyway.'

'Fair enough. I'm here.' Before following the Chief Inspector and the Sergeant he gave a vague wave in the direction of an oldish woman parked across the road in yet another Ford Escort, who had been anxiously watching what was happening.

CHAPTER 12

The telephone was ringing as the Chief Inspector led Paul Avery into his office. He gestured the doctor to a chair, and indicated that Greenway should remain with them. The phone call was brief.

'Dr Avery,' he said at once, putting down the receiver, 'the girl found in the Cherwell this morning is not Linda Jackson.'

'Not Linda? You're sure?'

'Yes. I've just heard that the body has been identified by her husband as that of Katerina or Kate Minden. There's no doubt. But keep it to yourself for the moment.'

'Thank God!' said Avery. 'I mean—I'm sorry for the girl, but thank God it's not Linda.'

Paul Avery buried his face in his hands, ashamed of his emotions, and Tansey seized his chance. 'Sergeant, phone the Rusts and the Jacksons, please. Just tell them that it's definitely not their daughter who was found in the river. Mrs Sherry should be told about Kate in person and, until that's done, everyone else can be left to guess.'

'Yes, sir. Would you—would you like me to go and tell Mrs Sherry?'

Tansey stared at his sergeant, and wondered why on earth he had ever considered her cold and distant. 'Thanks. I think she'd appreciate that.' He turned to Avery. 'Now, Doctor. There are a few questions.'

'Yes, Chief Inspector. I can imagine, but first—about the instructions you gave to your sergeant. Please may I tell Miss Foyne and Miss Gower that it's not Linda?'

'Miss Foyne and—?'

'Yes. You remember. She lives above us with Miss Gower, whom you met. It was Miss Foyne who drove me here. They're both awfully concerned about Linda.'

'I don't see why not,' said the Chief Inspector. 'Only make sure they don't spread the news around either.'

'Oh, that's great,' said Avery. 'They'll be so relieved, and—'

Tansey let Paul Avery talk, knowing he would find relief in words. But time was precious. He eyed his overflowing in-tray with distaste, and glanced obviously at his watch.

Avery took the hint. 'I'm sorry, Chief Inspector—I've been rabbiting on. I was so thankful it wasn't Linda who was dead that for a moment I almost forgot she was still missing. You said there were some questions?'

'Yes. The first is pretty obvious, I imagine.'

'Yes, I can guess. In my excitement outside I mentioned my wife. It's true. Linda's my wife. We've been married for a year. That's—that's what we were going to celebrate the night she disappeared.'

'At least that's one small mystery solved.' Dick Tansey grinned. 'But why keep it a secret?'

'It's simply a matter of money. Linda's dependent on her scholarships and grants. If it weren't for them, she wouldn't be up here at Oxford. There's one award in particular, which provides more than half her income; it's from a charitable trust and it would cease if it became known she was married. Of course, we didn't have to get married, but we wanted to, and now . . .' Avery's voice had roughened. 'It's the not knowing that's so ghastly. I've seen that with patients. They try to steel themselves against the worst, but they can't help hoping, and it tears them apart.'

Tansey was silent. There was nothing he could say that was worth while. It would be ludicrous to offer false hope. The best he could do was change the subject.

'What's your opinion of Quentin Wood?' he asked abruptly.

'Wood? I don't know him intimately. I've been to a few parties at his house, but that's all. Otherwise it's what Linda's told me about him, and some general gossip.'

'Such as—' Tansey prompted.

'He seems to me rather a mass of contradictions. Academically he's said to be brilliant, but he's lazy and he hasn't published as much as he might. On the other hand he takes a lot of trouble with his pupils. Linda thought—thinks—he's wonderful.'

'Did he ever make a pass at her?'

'No! Not to my knowledge.' Avery was surprised.

'Why not? She was—is—an exceptionally lovely girl, and I gather Wood has a reputation as a womanizer.'

'Probably deserved at some time, before or immediately after his divorce, but I gather that for some years now he's been seeing a lady who won't leave her crippled husband. Linda's met her, and says she's a very pleasant woman.'

'I see,' said Tansey, and thought this might account for Wood's abusive aversion to answering questions about his movements. 'Why did Linda refuse to pose for Wood? He's a first-class photographer, it seems.'

'I didn't know she—Oh, for heaven's sake, Chief Inspector, who on earth have you been talking to?' Avery caught back the denial he had been about to make. 'I remember

now. It was at one of Wood's parties. He said Linda reminded him of that Botticelli painting—you know, "Venus
rising from the foam", and would she let him take her like
that. It was only a joke. He didn't mean it. He knew she'd
refuse.'

'Ah! My informant was clearly wrong.'

'Chief Inspector, may I ask? Why all these questions
about Quentin Wood? You can't possibly suspect him of
anything. He's always been very good to Linda. He's one
of the few people who knows about our marriage.'

At this point there was a tap on the door, and a uniformed
officer poked his head round the door.

'I know you said you weren't to be interrupted, sir, but
there's a Mr Cyril Ewan on the phone, and he said it was
terribly urgent.'

'All right. I'll take it. Get it put through here, and find
someone to escort Dr Avery to the car that's waiting for him
outside.' Tansey nodded goodbye to the doctor. 'Dr Avery,
I'll let you know the moment there's any news of Linda—
good or bad.'

'Thanks. I'm most grateful.'

But Tansey was already reaching for the phone. 'Tansey
here. Is that Mr Ewan?'

'Yes, Cyril Ewan, but Tom's here with me.' The voice
was breathless, as if its owner was over-excited. 'Chief
Inspector, we've heard from him again—from that man
Browne. We received half a dozen pix in this morning's
post, the brunette and a new blonde girl, but no note with
it. Then he rang us up five minutes ago, a husky voice, kind
of false-sounding.'

'What did he say, Mr Ewan?'

'He told us to keep any money we owed him till he let us
know what to do with it. Meanwhile, he'd be sending us
some more pix for *Beautiful Butterflies*. But—but—' Cyril
Ewan stammered in his excitement. 'He said we were to
keep our noses clean, or else what happened to Gus Hunter

could happen to us. Chief Inspector, that means he'll kill us.'

Tom's voice broke in. 'We're asking for police protection, Chief Inspector.'

Tansey cursed under his breath. 'Mr Ewan, I can't offer you police protection, as you call it—we just haven't enough manpower for any effective surveillance. What's more, I don't believe it's necessary. I don't believe you or your son are in any great danger. We'll want to make copies of the pictures, as before—I'll send an officer to collect them right away. Then do what Browne tells you. Publish the photographs and keep the money till you get his instructions. Then let me know immediately. Immediately!'

There was muttering at the other end of the line. Clearly the Ewans were conferring together. Tansey wondered how far they could be trusted, and decided that it wasn't far. They'd cooperate with the police only if they feared a heavy fine and the end of *Beautiful Butterflies* more than they were scared of Browne's threats.

'Hello, Mr Tansey. You're there?' This was Tom Ewan.

'Yes, I'm still here, Mr Ewan,' said Tansey, 'though I've nothing more to add. I'm sure you've realized that the sensible thing to do is to help the police, who will be most appreciative. After all, you wouldn't want to be accused of conspiracy with Browne, would you? And if we can catch him he'll be put away where he can't do you any harm.'

Again there was a silence, but not for so long. 'You can count on us,' Cyril Ewan said at last. 'We'll be in touch as soon as this Browne contacts us, I promise you.'

'Thanks,' said Tansey, and hoped they meant it.

In the middle of the afternoon the pathologist telephoned. Tansey had attended the start of the PM, but had had to go before its completion, leaving another officer as witness. He was eagerly awaiting the final result.

The pathologist said, 'You'll get a full report on the late

Katerina Minden tomorrow, but I thought you'd like to have some facts right away.'

'Of course I'd be grateful,' said Tansey.

'I'll skip the bits about approximate age, well-nourished body, etc. You know them already.'

'Yes.' As always Tansey wondered how, given the nature of their work, pathologists could sound so cheerful.

'Here's the nitty-gritty then. Minden died of heart failure.'

'What?'

'Yes, I thought you'd be surprised. She wasn't drowned; there's no water in the lungs. Nor is there any sign of violence on her person—except for the face, of course—no bruising, or abrasions or anything like that. Incidentally, there's no indication of sexual abuse either, though she's been kept under sedation for a continuous period. I suspect an antipsychotic drug—a major tranquillizer, something like chlorpromazine in massive doses—but the test results aren't through yet.'

'But heart failure? Are you telling me she died a natural death?' Tansey refused to believe it.

'Yes and no.'

'What the hell does that mean?'

'In simple terms, the immediate cause of death was heart failure, as I said; I won't go into details now, but there are indications that her heart was abnormal—probably rheumatic fever as a child, or something like that, I would think. The most likely thing is that the failure was caused by shock—perhaps the shock of having acid thrown into her face.'

'You said "thrown". Could it conceivably have been an accident? A bottle knocked off a shelf, or something like that?'

'I should think it extremely improbable. The burning was so complete. If you want me to do your work for you, I'd say the girl was in a position where she couldn't dodge—under sedation, or backed up in a corner, perhaps.'

'Alternatively, the acid could have been thrown as a form of defence—if she seemed likely to attack.'

'Could be—from what you've told me of the background.'

'It makes more sense. Having carefully picked a beautiful girl off the street to pose for his photographs, he wouldn't purposely make her useless, would he?'

'Not unless he got tired of her, and intended to trade her in for a later model,' the pathologist said brutally.

'God forbid!' The possibility of an attempt to replace Kate had occurred to Tansey, but it was not a prospect he wanted to face. Now he reminded himself to ask the media to stress the need for all young women, especially those with long auburn hair, to be on their guard and take no risks. 'Is there anything else you want to tell me?' he asked.

'No. The rest can wait for my report.'

Tansey thanked the pathologist, and put down his receiver. At that moment Sergeant Greenway came into his office to report on her visit to Mrs Sherry, who had taken the frightful news with surprising calm. The sergeant had also remembered Tansey's instructions to investigate Mrs Wilton, and had discovered that Wood's housekeeper was a devout Catholic, and a most unlikely individual to assist in any such activities as those of the unidentified Browne.

In his turn, Tansey retailed the gist of the pathologist's report to her. She made one useful comment. If Kate Minden knew she had a weak heart, that might account for her eagerness to put as much money as possible by to support her child.

'That's certainly possible,' said the Chief Inspector. Then he picked up his phone again. The first priority was to make an appointment to see Quentin Wood as soon as he could.

Tansey arrived at Wood's house on the dot of five o'clock. The housekeeper, in a warm coat and carrying a bag, opened the door to him before he had a chance to ring the bell.

'I have an appointment to see Mr Wood. Detective Chief Inspector Tansey.'

'Yes, sir. I—I was just leaving.'

'It's okay, Mrs Wilton.' Quentin Wood came into the hall. 'Off you go. And don't come in tomorrow if your cold's no better.'

'Very good, sir. Thank you, and good night.'

Mrs Wilton bustled away, and Wood showed the Chief Inspector into the booklined workroom. To Tansey's relief, the photograph of the baby with the large pink bow was in the same place on the desk.

'Sit down, Chief Inspector, and tell me what you want. I've a pupil coming for a tutorial at five-thirty, so be as brief as you can, will you?'

'I'll do my best, sir.' There was an edge to Tansey's voice, but he restrained himself from reminding Wood that he represented the forces of law and order. Pupils could wait, if necessary.

He said, 'Perhaps you'd begin by telling me when you took that photograph of the beribboned baby.'

Quentin Wood stared at Tansey in open amazement. 'Are you crazy, Chief Inspector, or am I?'

'Neither of us, I trust, sir. Please just answer my question.'

'I'm not sure I could tell you the exact day—I don't keep meticulous records, the way some photographers do. But I took a lot of proofs of that baby. She's my first grandchild. My son or my daughter-in-law might remember when we did that one, if it's important. They've both been here a number of times recently, with the baby.'

Wood mentioned some dates. They were no help to Tansey. They neither confirmed that the photograph had been taken before the publication of the issue of *Beautiful Butterflies* in which Wood could have seen Kate Minden in a similar pose, nor did they prove that Minden's picture had been taken first.

'Would Mrs Wilton remember the occasion?'

Wood shook his head. 'No, I'm sure she wouldn't,' he said. Obviously, if he believed himself under suspicion in any way, he was in no hurry to clear himself. 'She might remember when I brought this enlargement up to my study, but she wouldn't know when I took the actual photograph.'

'What made you chose that particular pose, sir?'

'I told you. It's one of many. You don't know much about photography, do you, Chief Inspector?' Wood was becoming irritated. 'These days it's not just a question of telling the sitter to say cheese, popping underneath a black cloth and pressing a rubber bulb. There's a lot more to it than that, and children are particularly difficult. They're like—they *are*—small animals.'

'I see,' said Tansey. 'But that particular set-up. Someone must have planned it. That ribbon—you must have designed the picture. Was it an original idea?'

'My daughter-in-law produced the ribbon. The baby was getting bored, and it served as a distraction. Then she rolled around, and managed to get herself tied up in it. I suppose that gave me the idea. The traditional chocolate-box, you know, only more so. It may have been a bit naughty, but anyway we rearranged the ribbon and took the shot.' Wood frowned. He sounded doubtful, as if he didn't altogether believe what he had said.

'Do you ever see a magazine called *Beautiful Butterflies*, sir?'

'I've never even heard of it.'

'Right. Thank you, sir.' Tansey stood up. 'I think I heard a doorbell. That'll be your pupil.'

'You mean you're not going to tell me what this is all about? These absolutely bizarre questions—'

'No, sir. I'm sorry. I can't at the moment. And I'm going to ask you not to report our conversation to any third party. Please. It's important.'

'All right,' said Wood resignedly. 'If you say so, Chief Inspector.'

CHAPTER 13

Three days later Jane Sinclair disappeared. It happened in the early afternoon, and on this occasion there was no doubt about the timing, or the fact that it had been a bold and forceful abduction.

Jane Sinclair was twenty-five. She was another beautiful girl, petite, with green eyes, a creamy complexion—and long red hair. She lived with her husband, Bill, and her four-year-old daughter, Carol, in Wynford, a village not far from Abingdon, where Bill was the manager of a bookshop.

Each morning Bill drove his wife and daughter into Abingdon. He dropped them at the private nursery school, which Carol attended and where Jane assisted, before going on to park in a space behind his shop. Each afternoon, after Carol had rested while Jane took the opportunity to do some shopping or merely to relax, mother and daughter returned to Wynford by bus. Of necessity it was a long day for a four-year-old, but Pam Thornton, who ran the nursery school, had become a close friend of the Sinclairs, and the routine worked well.

Pam had been trained as a nursery school teacher, and her present establishment was very conveniently located in her own home. Her house was ideal for its purpose. It was large and Victorian, set in a quiet residential street with a minimum of through traffic, and well-separated from its neighbours. The school's activities took place on the ground floor while Pam and her husband lived on the floors above.

Even before the disappearance of Kate Minden, Jane would never have accepted a lift from a stranger. Since the incidents had multiplied, Bill Sinclair had been particularly insistent that she should never, never enter a car—unless someone like Pam Thornton was driving it.

'The devil probably lives in or around Oxford, and he's got a car,' Sinclair said. 'It may be a Ford Escort, as the papers suggest, or it may not. As far as I can tell, unless they're keeping very quiet, the police don't have a clue, and they know damn-all about him. Jane, he could be anyone —the vicar, or the old farmer where you buy eggs sometimes, or—or the publican at the Greyhound. So, don't take any risks.'

Jane Sinclair had laughed at the possible criminals her husband had listed, but she certainly had no intention of taking risks. She was much too sensible and, though she didn't believe that any such tragedy could happen to her, the reports of Kate's mutilated body had caused her a tremor of apprehension.

On this particular day it had rained steadily since dawn and by lunch-time, with the sky grey and lowering, it had become necessary to turn on the lights in the nursery school. After lunch the children who had not yet been collected by their parents lay on mattresses on the floor to rest. Usually they went to sleep quickly, but today the rain and the unexpected darkness seemed to have disturbed them, and they took a while to settle.

When at last they were quiet Jane said, 'Pam, will it be all right if I pop out to the shops now? I need to buy some lamb chops, and one or two other things.'

'Of course. You know you don't have to ask. But it's a dreadful day. Do you really have to go, Jane?'

'Yes, I must. I shan't be long, and I've got my raincoat and an umbrella.'

Pam Thornton, ten years older than Jane, with her own children away at school and her husband frequently abroad on business, had grown fond of the young Sinclairs. She stood at the window, and watched Jane—a slight figure, head bent in shelter behind her big multi-coloured golf umbrella—hurry along the almost deserted road, and turn down the pedestrian alleyway that led between the houses.

This alleyway was a well-known short cut to a nearby street about fifty yards away where a most useful scattering of small shops had somehow managed to survive.

As soon as Jane turned into the alley, Pam went into the kitchen to make herself an extra cup of coffee. Thus she failed to see the car move. The Ford Escort, which had for some time been parked several houses away, drew out from the kerb and drove along the road until it was beside the entrance to the alleyway. There it stopped again and waited.

Jane was completing her shopping—chops, fresh vegetables, fruit. She tried to feed her family well but, except at weekends, she had little time for cooking, and usually found herself buying good, simple, but expensive food. Now she hesitated over the grapefruit. They were a dreadful price, but Carol loved them. Eventually she bought one.

Outside the greengrocer's she struggled against the wind and the lashing rain to put up her umbrella. Once she had achieved this, she did her best to move rapidly, plodding heedlessly through the puddles in her eagerness to reach the shelter and warmth of Pam Thornton's house. But she was laden with her purchases and buffeted by the weather, and made relatively slow progress. She scarcely noticed that the street was practically empty, and the alleyway completely so when she entered it.

She had almost reached the far end of the alleyway when she became conscious of someone coming towards her. Underneath the rim of her umbrella, which she was holding in front of her as some protection against the wind whistling through the narrow passage, she saw two brown shoes, the bottoms of grey slacks, a fawn raincoat. Then the umbrella was knocked roughly from her grasp.

'So sorry,' a deep voice said.

For a moment Jane was convinced it had been an accident. She almost smiled but, looking up at the face above her, its mouth grim and its eyes hard, she knew the attack had been intentional. She opened her mouth to scream.

At once a large gloved hand was clamped over her face. She tried to bite it, but her teeth had no effect on the thick leather of the glove. At the same time she kicked out with all her might, and had the satisfaction of hearing a grunt as her shoe connected with a shinbone.

But her struggle was pointless. She felt herself picked up, carried a yard or two, then thrown brutally on to the floor in the rear of a car. Her assailant followed her in and slammed the door. Immediately, the car moved forward and gathered speed, and the voice, no longer apologetic but now threatening, said, 'Lie still and keep quiet or you'll get this bottle of acid in that beautiful face of yours.'

Jane shivered involuntarily. She thought of her husband Bill in his bookshop, of little Carol and Pam Thornton at the nursery school, and absurdly she remembered the expensive grapefruit now lying somewhere in the alley. But there was nothing she could do, no action she could take. A light wool rug was thrown over her and, as ordered, she lay quiet beneath it, hoping and praying she was not to share Kate Minden's fate.

Pam Thornton was at a loss. She was a competent woman who had faced many crises, but this situation was new to her. She couldn't believe that Jane had been kidnapped— not during that short walk to the shops and back. She expected her to return at any moment, but each time she looked at the clock and assured Carol that Mummy would be back soon, her fears grew.

By four o'clock she could no longer deceive herself. All the children had been collected, and her other assistant had left hours ago to visit her dentist, but there was still no sign of Jane. Pam bundled Carol into her outdoor clothes, put on a raincoat and tied a scarf around her hair.

'We're going to look for your mummy,' she said firmly.

Outside it was still wet and windy and cold. The child,

sensing that something was wrong, clung to Pam's hand and, too frightened to cry, began to whimper. A van drove past, sending a spray of water over the pavement, and Pam swore silently as it splashed her legs. Otherwise the road was deserted.

When they reached the entrance to the alleyway, Pam hesitated. There was a little light from the street at the other end, but the passage itself was dark and shadowy. Yet she had seen Jane turn down here, and it was the way Jane should have returned. Nevertheless, it was not inviting and Carol hung back.

'Come on, Carol dear,' Pam said, as much to encourage herself as the child.

'Ball! Ball!' said Carol pointing.

Pam peered in the direction Carol was indicating. The object she saw dimly was round and yellow, not a ball but a grapefruit. And lying not far from it was a single lamb chop spattered with mud. Lamb chop, remembered Pam Thornton at once, and she looked around for other signs of Jane's shopping. There were none, and the coloured umbrella was also missing. Pam picked Carol up in her arms.

'It's too horrid to be out,' she said, as casually as she could, hoping the child wouldn't notice the gruffness of her voice. 'Let's get back home into the warm.'

Carol went willingly and, once in the house, allowed her outdoor clothes to be removed. She was quiet now, as if Pam's fear had communicated itself to her. Pam carried her upstairs to the Thorntons' private quarters, took off her wet shoes and socks, wrapped her in a rug and gave her a book to look at.

'I'm going to get us both a hot drink and something to eat,' she said with assumed cheerfulness.

She went straight to the room that Charles Thornton used as a study. Wishing that her husband had been at home to support her, and not conducting his business in Germany, she telephoned Bill's bookshop. An assistant fetched Sinclair.

Pam was blunt; she could think of no way of explaining the situation tactfully. Nevertheless, at first Bill seemed unable to comprehend what she was suggesting.

'Bill,' Pam said finally, 'I'm going to phone the police. I won't call the local station. I'll try and get hold of Chief Inspector Tansey.'

'Tansey? Why Tansey?'

Pam realized that his question merely represented a refusal to accept the facts; Bill Sinclair read the papers and understood perfectly well why Tansey was the man. She said, 'I wish you'd make an effort to get along here as quickly as you can, Bill. Carol's quite safe, but she'll be glad to see you, and the police will want to talk to you.'

There was a long pause. Then, 'Yes, yes, I suppose you're right,' Bill Sinclair admitted miserably. 'I'll be there as soon as I can make it. But—Dear God! I—I still can't believe it.'

Tansey was in the Chief Constable's office. He was sitting excessively upright. His mouth was set.

'Yes, sir. Of course I understand.'

Philip Midvale suppressed a sigh. He was a highly intelligent man, and it would have been obvious to a moron that the Chief Inspector did *not* understand, and had no wish to understand, no intention of understanding. Midvale shifted his heavy body as if to make himself more comfortable, and regarded Tansey shrewdly for a moment before he tried again.

'Chief Inspector, I'm not criticizing you in any way. You seem to be doing everything possible, but—'

'Obviously Mr Rust doesn't agree with you, sir.'

'Forget Mr Rust. He's got a fixation. He's convinced that the young butcher—what's his name? Brian Quayle—raped Mary, and buried her body in Copley Wood. He won't be content till we've dug up every damned bush and tree.'

'We could tell him his daughter's alive and posing for pornographic photographs, sir,' remarked Tansey, who had recovered some of his equanimity.

The Chief Constable laughed. 'From what I gather, the man Rust would consider that a fate worse than getting murdered. However, as I was saying, Chief Inspector, the trouble is that we've had no positive results so far, in a case that's getting wide publicity.'

Tansey remained silent. He could have pointed out that he had discovered why three young women had mysteriously disappeared, had produced a tenable theory as to why Kate Minden had died, and had some proof that the petty black-mailer, Gus Hunter, had been murdered by 'Browne'.

The trouble was that, in spite of suspicions, he was no nearer to evidence that would put an identity to 'Browne'. It was not his fault, the Chief Inspector reflected, that the investigations of these crimes had demanded a great deal of manpower. And Browne had had the devil's own luck.

'—so you see my point, Chief Inspector,' Philip Midvale was saying. 'It's not that I don't have faith in your abilities, but theoretically, now we know it's a murder investigation —if not a multiple-murder case—and one with these un-pleasant overtones which make it a tabloid reporter's de-light, quite apart from the possibility that a fresh mind on the subject might be a good idea, there's every reason why I should put a superintendent in over-all charge.'

'Yes, sir,' said Tansey woodenly.

'Don't take it like that, Dick. You appreciate the problem as well as I do. And you know as well as I do that there isn't a superintendent immediately available anyway. So you'll just have to continue to do your best for the time being, and make sure the families concerned, as well as the media, realize that we're taking the case very seriously indeed. That's all we can do for the present.'

The telephone saved Tansey from the need for an immedi-

ate response, but the sight of Midvale's face was enough to
warn him what was coming.

'More bad news, I'm afraid, Chief Inspector.' Midvale
put down the receiver. 'Another girl has disappeared. In
Abingdon. One Jane Sinclair. Apparently she went out to
do a little shopping early this afternoon and hasn't been
seen since. Sergeant Greenway has the details.'

'Thank you, sir.' Tansey was already on his feet. He was
appalled at the report, but maybe one more disappearance
would provide a key to the case. Browne's luck couldn't last
for ever.

CHAPTER 14

'It's ludicrous! How dare he tear you off a strip, however
politely! He seems to think you've not done a damn thing,
though no one could have done more!' Sergeant Greenway
swallowed her indignation, and remembered the Chief Inspector's rank. 'I'm sorry, sir. I shouldn't have spoken out
like that. I apologize.'

'Don't be an idiot!'

The words were spoken with such affection that Hilary
Greenway, surprised, felt the colour rise in her cheeks. She
had known that her relationship with Dick Tansey was
undergoing a change. She had realized this first when she
found herself thinking about him, worrying about him. But
it was only very recently that she had come to accept that
she was falling in love with him. To relieve her feelings she
pressed her car horn hard.

'What was that for?' Tansey asked idly.

'I thought the car ahead was going to turn,' she lied.

'Oh! I thought perhaps—' Tansey said, and then stopped
abruptly.

They were on their way to Abingdon to interview Pam

Thornton and Bill Sinclair at the nursery school. The rain had eased a little, but it was so dark that the sergeant was driving on her lights. Sitting beside her, Tansey was becoming schizophrenic. On the one hand he was feeling guilty that he had confided in her his annoyance at the Chief Constable's suggestion that the case should be turned over to a Superintendent; on the other hand he knew he was glad he had done so, and he appreciated her reaction.

'It was a good idea to ask at once for a description of Jane Sinclair,' he said, 'and to bring along a photograph of Kate Minden for comparison.'

'I remembered that coach driver at Gloucester Green saying that there weren't many girls who looked like Kate, but Jane sounds very like her. What I don't understand is how Browne found her so quickly.'

'Chance, perhaps. Presumably he's been searching for a substitute since Kate died, and he was lucky. Or he could have spotted Jane long ago, but found it simpler to take Kate. Or he keeps a list of beautiful girls with long hair.'

Tansey shrugged. 'At least, because of the resemblance, we can be pretty sure we're dealing with Browne again, and not some joker who's taken to copying him. Unfortunately the media are certain to note the likeness, too, and it's not going to be long before they sniff out the pornographic angle. In fact, I'm astonished it hasn't surfaced already.'

'Would that really matter, sir? Might it not help?'

'It would certainly cause even more of a furore in the tabloids, and the families wouldn't like that. Mr Rust would probably die of shame. I know we'll have to issue a statement sometime, but publicity could frighten Browne off the Ewans, and they're the only contact we've got with him – whoever he is.'

'Perhaps Browne made a mistake over this last abduction,' Greenway suggested hopefully. 'Someone may have seen something this time.'

Tansey was not hopeful. 'On a day like this, and with our luck? What do you bet?'

'I'm not a betting woman, sir,' said Greenway primly, and had the satisfaction of seeing Tansey smile.

Pam Thornton opened her front door to them before they had time to knock. She greeted them with relief when they introduced themselves, and quietly showed them upstairs into her husband's study.

'I thought we'd have a word alone first, Chief Inspector. Bill, Jane's husband, is in the sitting-room with their little girl. He's shocked and appalled, just as I am. You can see him later, but he knows nothing. He was in his bookshop when Jane disappeared.'

'We'll need to see him, nevertheless, Mrs Thornton,' Tansey said, 'but perhaps you'd tell us what you know yourself.'

Considering the stress under which she was struggling, Pam Thornton told her story clearly and succinctly. What was more, she knew the exact time that Jane Sinclair had left the house. This meant that once the police had checked what Jane had bought, and made sure that the grapefruit and the chop had been part of her shopping, they could almost pinpoint the moment of the crime.

After a brief word with Bill Sinclair, who was pale but composed but could give them no help, except to produce from his wallet a colour photograph of his wife, they left the house. There was no need to comment on the likeness between Jane Sinclair and Kate Minden; the two girls could easily have been sisters.

'I'll look at this alleyway and check on the shops. They should still be open,' Tansey said. 'You phone in and get some officers to help with the routine—we must tape off the alley and start a proper search. Then there are the neighbours. I should think they might be a good bet. Browne must have parked around here for some while. He can't

have known when, or even if, Mrs Sinclair would go out on
a day like this, though she seems to have made a practice
of doing her shopping about this time. Someone must have
seen the car, if not its occupant or occupants. You'd better
start on the nearer houses yourself.'

'It's a very quiet road, sir. There wouldn't have been
many people about in this weather.'

'I know. Still, we can but try. Our Browne does manage
to seize opportunities, but his blasted luck's got to break
sometime.'

The Chief Inspector went in one direction, towards the
alleyway and the shops, and after using the car radio,
Sergeant Greenway started ringing doorbells. Tansey learnt
little. Jane Sinclair was well known in the small area, and
it took only a few minutes to establish that she had bought
three chops and some stewing steak at the butcher's, and
some vegetables and a grapefruit at the greengrocer's. She
had been carrying a shopping-bag, and a big coloured
umbrella. Both seemed to be missing; at least they weren't
to be found in the alleyway, where the chop and the grapefruit were all that remained.

It wasn't difficult for Tansey to reconstruct the crime, but
he discovered nothing that might help to identify Browne.
Disconsolately he returned to his car. Sergeant Greenway
had not yet reappeared, so Tansey busied himself with
making a list and phoning it through to Headquarters. To
hell with the personnel problem, he thought. He needed to
know where everyone concerned had been between noon
and four that day. At least firm alibis might exonerate some
of them—though he reminded himself that Browne could
well be missing from the list.

He had scarcely finished his call when there was a warning
tap on the car window, and Greenway opened the door. She
got in beside him.

'I think I may have struck lucky, sir,' she said.

'Good girl. That's more than I have.'

'There's a boy at No. 7 along the road. He's twelve and he's intelligent. He should have been at school, but he's got a frightful cold, so his mother kept him at home and in his room. He was bored, and spent a lot of the afternoon staring out of the window. His room's upstairs, so he had a good view.'

'Don't tell me he saw the whole thing.'

'Not quite. He saw Jane Sinclair go down the road. He doesn't know her, but he described her struggling against the wind and the rain with her big golf umbrella. He says that as she turned into the alley a blue Ford Escort that had been parked opposite his house moved slowly along until it stopped again opposite the entrance to the alley.'

Greenway, who had been speaking rapidly, paused for breath. For a moment Tansey was disappointed. Their belief that Browne drove a blue Ford Escort was confirmed, but that didn't help much.

'Is that all, Sergeant?'

'It is not, sir! The boy saw the same car there on Monday, as he was coming home from school. Like today, there was one person in the back and a driver in the front. As he passed, the one in the back was picking something up off the floor—and conveniently hiding his face at the same time —but the boy did see the driver. It was a woman, he says. He describes her as old, perhaps sixty. She had a woollen cap pulled down over her ears, but he was able to see some white hair.'

'An observant lad. Of course some people go white early in life. Did you ask him if he'd recognize this woman again?'

'I did, and he said he would, especially if she scowled at him as she did on Monday.'

'That's splendid. Except that I can't think of any white-haired women who might fit his description—except for Mrs Sherry, Kate's mother.'

Greenway was amused. 'I can't visualize Mrs Sherry helping to take pornographic pictures, sir. Maybe we've not met Browne's car driver yet—nor, for that matter, Browne himself.'

'I was thinking the same thing myself, but—I hate to admit it, but I've a nasty gut feeling that somewhere I've missed something,' Tansey said. 'The Chief Constable's got a point. It won't do any harm to go through the case again from the beginning.'

'There's something else, sir,' said Greenway.

'Don't tell me this young genius of yours took the number of the Escort?'

'Not quite that,' said Greenway. 'But he noticed that the number plate was very dirty, so that it was hard to read, though the rest of the car was clean.'

'That follows, though it would have been more sensible not to clean the rest of the car too well.'

'That's true. But at least it made the boy take an interest, and inspect it carefully. He's almost sure the first letter was last year's registration letter, and that the first of the following figures was a four.'

'That's great,' said Tansey, seized with a momentary enthusiasm. 'I'm not sure, but I think that computer at the motor vehicles licensing place in Swansea could come up with something on the basis of all this. A Ford Escort— blue—first registered last year, presumably in the Oxford- shire area—with a four as the initial figure. Anyway, it's worth trying. A print-out of all such cars might show up some interesting names. You never know.'

Tansey lifted the phone again, and spoke to Headquarters rapidly and demandingly. Then he looked at his watch. 'Meanwhile, seeing as how it's such a filthy day, I think we'll find a decent pub and treat ourselves to a drink before going back to Kidlington. Is that all right with you—Sergeant?

'Sir—' She mocked him. 'That would be smashing.'

Dick Tansey worked until late that night, checking files, making lists, going through his own and Sergeant Greenway's notes yet again, trying to take a fresh view of the case. It was not easy. But the results intrigued him.

He had listed all those concerned with the crimes, however remotely or vaguely, and was surprised that the cast of characters was so lengthy. And, in spite of the vast amount of investigation that had taken place, in spite of the very many questions asked and answered, he could now see that there were large areas which had not yet been explored.

For instance, Mrs Sherry was not the only white-haired old lady involved. Miss Gower, who lived in the same house as Linda Jackson, fitted the description but, for all he knew, she didn't drive. Then the wife of Knight, the estate agent, had turned out to be an almost platinum blonde, so that she could possibly be mistaken for white-haired. And, come to that, Cyril Ewan with a woollen cap pulled low might well be taken for a white-haired woman.

Tansey sighed and stretched. He was tired. It had been a long, dreary day, the one bright interval the time he had spent drinking with Sergeant Greenway. He let his thoughts wander, thinking of might-have-beens, and pulled himself together with a jerk. At least, thanks to the inquiries he had initiated, something had been achieved and some possible suspects eliminated.

Brian Quayle had been working in the butcher's shop in Colombury all the afternoon. Dr Paul Avery had been assisting at an operation in the Radcliffe Infirmary. Tony Knight had been showing houses to a pair of prospective clients, who could vouch for him though they were slightly uncertain of exact times. Neither Quayle nor Avery, therefore, could conceivably have had a hand in the abduction of Jane Sinclair. Knight might have done, but the distances were such as to make it ninety-nine per cent improbable.

Nevertheless, the next morning the Chief Inspector went straight from his home to the estate agency, outside which stood a blue Ford Escort. Knight was in his office going through the day's appointments with a new girl—not the

Temp—who had taken Kate Minden's place permanently. Cousin had not yet arrived. Knight looked tired and harassed, and he was not welcoming.

'What do you want now, Chief Inspector? Your minions are constantly bothering me. Believe me, Kate was the last person I'd have hurt. I didn't realize how much the business depended on her until we—we lost her.'

Tansey produced a casual apology. 'Mr Knight, you drive a station wagon on business, I know. Do you have another car?'

'Me? Good heavens, no. Can't afford it.'

'But your wife has a car?'

'Oh yes. That Ford Escort outside. It was a present from her father last January. He's in the motor business. You can ask her about it yourself if you like. She's upstairs. But why are you interested?'

Tansey didn't answer directly. Instead, he said, 'Would your wife have been in Abingdon yesterday afternoon?'

To Tansey's surprise, Knight's new secretary answered. 'No. She was here all the afternoon. Mr Knight and Mr Cousin were both out, and Mrs Knight was showing me the ropes—the filing system, and how to choose the right properties to suggest to clients, so that they aren't bothered with masses of unsuitable ones, and things like that. I've only been here a few days,' she added by way of explanation.

Tansey's interest subsided. 'I suppose Mrs Knight wouldn't lend her car to anyone, would she?' he asked tentatively.

Knight laughed. 'You must be joking. She'll hardly let me drive it. So if you're looking for a Ford Escort in Abingdon, it's not my wife's.'

And there goes one line of inquiry, Tansey thought. If Cousin was Browne, his companion was not the fair-haired Mrs Knight. Both the Knights were in the clear. But his theory that the girls might be prisoners in an empty house to which only the estate agents held keys, still held good. He said goodbye to Knight and the secretary and, as he was leaving the agency, met Peter Cousin outside on the pavement.

'I see from the papers that you've lost another girl,' said Cousin, 'and again, as you've already discovered, I don't have an alibi.'

To Tansey Cousin's manner sounded facetious. 'I find neither of those facts very amusing, Mr Cousin,' he said icily. He pointed at a white Rover, which he recognized as Cousin's. 'Incidentally, is that the only car you own?'

Cousin was surprised. 'Yes, it is! And I *don't* find what's happening to those girls very amusing either. Not seeing that Kate was one of them, anyway. I told you before, and I'll tell you again, Tansey. I loved Kate Minden, though she wouldn't look at me, and why should she? Make what you like of that.'

Abruptly Cousin turned and limped hurriedly into the agency, leaving Tansey to stare after him. It was difficult to believe that Cousin's outburst was other than genuine and yet . . . Not for the first time Tansey remembered that the witness who had seen Browne leave Gus Hunter's shop on the night the little blackmailer was killed thought that Browne had limped. But even with the best of intentions, witnesses were often in error.

CHAPTER 15

It was Monday afternoon before Chief Inspector Tansey made any further progress, though it was not for want of effort in the interval.

On Friday he had attended the inquest on Mrs Katerina Minden, which had been opened and immediately adjourned after evidence of identification had been given. He had prepared a statement for the public, naming neither *Beautiful Butterflies* nor its publishers, but suggesting that it was believed the missing girls were being used as models for pornographic photographs, and possibly films. The statement had not been easy to draft, and had subsequently brought down on Tansey a storm of inquiries both from the families of the girls and from the press, television and radio, all demanding more detailed information—and, in some obvious cases, copies of the allegedly pornographic pictures.

Not least concerned among those who saw the statement were Cyril and Tom Ewan. Tansey had spent Monday morning in court, giving evidence against Steve Minden who, accused of assaulting the police as well as failing to report to his probation officer, had been sent to prison for another six months. On his return to Headquarters after lunch the Chief Inspector found urgent messages to phone the Ewans. Tom answered on the second ring.

'Ah, it's you, Chief Inspector. At last. We've been trying to get in touch with you all day. We've heard from Browne again. He's very angry with us, and threatening. He blames us for all that stuff in the papers and on the box. Dad's dreadfully upset. He didn't want me to ring you—or have anything else to do with the police—but I persuaded him.'

'That was sensible of you, Mr Ewan,' said Tansey. 'Did Browne phone or write?'

'Both. That's to say, he phoned, but he also sent us some more pix with orders to print them in the next edition of *Butterflies*. We'll do it, because you told us to do as he said, Chief Inspector, but my father thinks they're a bit—er—strong.' Tom Ewan sounded anxious, as if he feared Tansey might have changed his mind, and was prepared to put the Ewans, father and son, at risk, by refusing to let them continue to carry out Browne's instructions. 'But you'll want someone to see them first, won't you?'

Tansey had intended to pay a surprise visit to the Ewans, and ask to look over the printing plant. He blamed himself for not having done so already. Whatever the Ewans might pretend, they were interested in pornography—or at least in the money it made—and it was hard to think of them as shocked or disgusted by the stuff they published. Apparently their staff was small—modern technology made this possible in the printing trade—and it was just possible that the nature of the premises would allow them to keep girls there, under sedation, without anyone knowing. Their alibis for the afternoon on which Jane Sinclair had been abducted were flimsy, dependent on each other, and Tansey found it easy to visualize Cyril with a woollen hat pulled well down over his face. If the whole idea seemed preposterous, it was no more so than any other scenario he could imagine.

'I'll be along myself,' he said, 'probably late this afternoon.'

In fact, the Chief Inspector and Sergeant Greenway set off for Reading almost at once. But if Tansey hoped to surprise the Ewans, he was disappointed. They seemed genuinely glad to see him, though less pleased by the presence of the sergeant; the reason for this soon became clear. Tom took them into Cyril's inner sanctum, and produced the most recent batch of transparencies.

There were half a dozen. Tom Ewan laid them out one by one on the light box in front of the Chief Inspector, positioning himself so as to shield Greenway from the pictures. He held the slides by the edges of their mounts, as was normal, but to judge from Browne's past care there was little hope of fingerprints.

'You see—they make a kind of story,' Cyril Ewan said. 'They're wicked, blasphemous. We'd never use stuff like this normally. I don't think the young lady—' He nodded towards Sergeant Greenway.

'Don't be silly, Mr Ewan,' Tansey said. 'My sergeant has to see all the evidence. It won't shock her.'

Cyril Ewan shrugged, and once he had seen the transparencies Tansey realized what he meant. He wouldn't have called himself a religious man, but for once he himself was slightly shocked. The redhead—Jane Sinclair—appeared in all six pictures. In the first two she was masturbating excitedly. In the third she had a pink cushion tied to her abdomen to suggest that she was pregnant, though without male intervention. In the fourth she was greeted obscenely but with apparent reverence by the brunette—Mary Rust —and in the fifth the blonde—Linda Jackson—took Mary's place. The sixth showed the three girls together in attitudes of abandoned exhaustion.

'He's getting bolder, our Mr Browne,' Tansey said. 'He hasn't taken as much trouble as usual to hide the faces, but of course by now he knows we know what he's up to.'

'And he blames us,' Cyril Ewan said. 'On the telephone he said that something terrible would happen to us. I'm afraid he'll set fire to the works, or shoot a member of our families.'

'I think the time's come when I'd better try to arrange some protection for you, Mr Ewan,' said Tansey, thinking that the bolder Browne became the more likely he was to make a mistake. 'You kept the envelope these came in, I'm glad to see.' He held out his hand for the thick manilla envelope Tom was still holding. 'May I have it, please?'

'It's postmarked Oxford, like last time,' Tom said, passing it over. 'And our name and address are typed, but the numbers are handwritten. He couldn't type those, could he?'

'What numbers?'

'Those there—on the backs of the cardboard mounts of the transparencies, to show what order they should go in.'

Carefully Tansey turned over the slides. As Tom Ewan had said, they had been numbered from one to six with a black grease pencil. Tansey could see nothing distinctive about the numerals, but by the number '5' there was a small, reddish-brown mark, and a similar, but larger stain,

appeared across the edge of number '6'. The Chief Inspector
peered at the marks.

'Were those stains here when the photographs arrived,
Mr Ewan?'

'Yes. I don't know what they are.'

'I think they're blood,' said Tansey. 'It looks to me as if
Browne, or whoever was numbering the slides, cut his finger
without noticing immediately, and then didn't consider the
marks worth bothering about.'

'He was right,' said Tom Ewan. 'They don't matter, for
they're not on the transparencies themselves, see?'

'They certainly could matter,' Tansey said thoughtfully.
'They might help us to catch Browne—or at least help to
prove his guilt when we do catch him. Haven't you heard
of blood groups, Mr Ewan? Forensic scientists can do wonderful things these days. I shall have to take these slides
with me, Mr Ewan. I'll copy them, as I did before.'

'You'll send us back the originals as soon as possible,
Chief Inspector,' said Tom Ewan. 'We're up against a fairly
tight deadline for the next issue of *Butterflies*, and if we don't
include them Browne might act.'

'I see your point,' said Tansey, 'but there's a problem.
These bloodstains—if they are bloodstains—on numbers
"5" and "6" may be evidence, which means we'll have to
keep the slides. But I'll do my best to get our lab to make
sure the copies are indistinguishable from the originals. Will
that satisfy you?'

'It'll have to,' said Cyril Ewan resignedly.

'And before we go,' added Tansey, 'we'd like to see over
your printing plant.'

Cyril Ewan agreed at once. 'Why not, if you wish. Tom
will show you round. We've nothing to hide from you, Mr
Tansey.'

In fact, the two officers were able to make a thorough if
inconspicuous inspection of the premises of Ewan & Son,

Printers and Publishers. Clearly Tom was proud of the works and the modern equipment, and the merest indication of interest was sufficient to make him open up storerooms and point out every nook and cranny of the place. Unless they were extremely clever, it was as Cyril had said—they had nothing to hide from the police—except of course their pornographic operations. The photographic, plating and printing equipment for this aspect of their work appeared to be completely separate from their more mundane jobs and, as far as Tansey and Greenway could see, Tom Ewan was telling the truth when he said that only two men, with his own personal assistance, were employed here. In any case, there was no sign that the missing girls had ever been anywhere near the establishment, and there were no apparent facilities for keeping them there.

'That was a waste of time,' Tansey said, as they started to drive back to Kidlington. 'Inspecting the works, I mean. But the dried blood on those slides could prove useful.'

'Yes, sir.' Greenway was smiling broadly.

'What's amusing you, Sergeant?'

'I was thinking of Cyril Ewan's concern for my feelings, sir, and Tom Ewan's remark that the main reason they kept the pornography segregated from the rest of the business was because it wouldn't have been nice for the ladies working on greetings cards and religious publications and so on to know about it. He gave me a very pointed look then. Obviously porn is for men only—and, of course, the girls they use.'

Tansey grinned. 'Yes. They're an awful pair of hypocrites are Cyril and Tom, but, having talked to them again, I can't see them as Browne and company. Can you?'

'No, I can't. They don't fit *my* conception of Browne and his helpmeet, at any rate.'

'How do you think of them?'

'Browne is someone who hates women, beautiful women, probably because there's something wrong with him, either physically or psychologically and so he's been spurned by them, as they used to say in old novels. Or he thinks he has.' Sergeant Greenway was speaking slowly. 'Making them model for dirty pictures could easily be a form of revenge.'

Tansey nodded. 'Yes, I'd agree with that. But it doesn't help much, does it?'

'It helps to eliminate some of our possibles, if only marginally,' Greenway said.

Tansey glanced sideways at her, and sighed. 'I've a horrible feeling that we'll end by eliminating them all, and when a superintendent takes over the case he'll find a completely different couple of villains.'

If this was a plea for encouragement, Sergeant Greenway ignored it. 'And this Browne's got some kind of complex about hair,' she continued. 'It's not just that all the girls he's grabbed have beautiful long hair; to me the fact that Kate was shaved so completely is even more significant.'

'He's also a superb photographer, no matter what you think of his subjects. From what I'm told by experts he might have been in the top ten.' Tansey paused. 'So, does anyone else come to mind, Sergeant?'

'Quentin Wood—because of the photography. And I'm not entirely happy with his explanation about how he came to take that picture of the baby with the bow round its middle. Can the similar photo of Kate merely be coincidence?' Greenway said at once. 'But he couldn't keep the girls in his house without the housekeeper knowing—and he doesn't own a Ford Escort. You say his lady friend is beyond reproach, sir, but he might have another one—' She broke off, and forced herself to laugh. 'I'm not exactly describing someone with a grudge against women, am I?'

'Scarcely. I could argue that Peter Cousin fits the bill better. He may have been in love with Kate, but he doesn't seem to have got anywhere with her. He's a pretty good photographer, too, and he might have access to an empty house somewhere near Oxford that we know nothing about. Or his helper could own the house—and the Ford Escort. Why does Browne have to drive such a popular make of car? Damn him!' Tansey swore gently. 'I've—we've—been over all this times without number, and we get no further. I was hoping Jane Sinclair's disappearance might bring us nearer to Browne, but we've had no results so far.'

'There are the bloodstains on those slides, sir,' Greenway reminded the Chief Inspector. 'You know what the forensic people are like—it's not just grouping nowadays. We shall probably have to ask some of the possibles—Wood and Cousin, say—for samples. That should please them.'

'Oh hell, I give up,' said Tansey finally. 'To some extent making anything of that blood—if it is blood, and with our luck it's more likely to be strawberry jam—depends on our having already met Browne in another guise, and for that matter his helper, who could equally well have cut his or her finger. It's just too wretchedly complex.'

'Yes, sir,' said Sergeant Greenway meekly.

When the Chief Inspector reached his office he found on top of his in-tray a batch of computer print-outs. Someone in Swansea had managed to persuade their machine to produce a listing of Ford Escorts that met the criteria Tansey had outlined. What was more, it had sorted the registered owners by alphabetical order of surnames.

Tansey gave the Swansea authorities full marks. It was a long list, but almost the first name to catch his eye was that of Peter Cousin. The Chief Inspector checked rapidly through the rest of the print-out. He noted the names of Mrs Knight, the wife of the estate agent, of Mr Quayle, Brian's father, and someone who might be the husband of Quentin Wood's housekeeper.

He gave orders that Peter Cousin should be found immediately, and politely invited to visit Headquarters, but when an irate Cousin eventually arrived, he kept him wait-

ing in a bare interrogation room for twenty minutes. Cousin
was angry.

'What the hell's all this about?' he demanded. 'Not only
are you wasting my time, Chief Inspector, but you may well
have lost me a sale. I had to cancel an appointment with a
client who was on the verge of closing—all because of you.'

'You've been wasting *my* time—and the taxpayer's
money, too, Mr Cousin,' Tansey said. 'You denied owning
a second car, when in fact since last April you've owned a
Ford Escort—'

'No!'

'You deny owning—'

'No, I own it, all right. But you asked me if I ran another
car, and I told you the literal truth. It's like this.'

According to Cousin, though he was not a great betting
man, he occasionally had a flutter, and he had made some
money on the horses last spring. At the same time he had
been offered an almost new car, whose previous owner had
died. He didn't particularly need the car, but he had bought
it and then immediately given it to his sister on a long
loan.

'Her husband had just lost his job, and with it his company
car, and they were completely without transport. It was no
joke, as they live in the depths of the country and they've
got three kids. I'd have given them the Ford, but they
wouldn't let me, so nominally it's mine but they use it all
the time and I think of it as theirs.'

It was a rational explanation, and easy to check, though
checked it would be. For the moment Tansey accepted it as
the truth, but even so it didn't put Cousin entirely in the
clear.

'You drive the Ford yourself sometimes?' the Chief Inspector asked.

'I have done. I borrowed it for a day or two a few weeks
ago when my own car was on the blink.'

'What colour is it?'

'Grey. Blue-grey. These metallic paints look different in different lights. But what—'

'Tell me about your sister.'

'What d'you want to know about her? She's actually my half-sister. She's in her early forties and a very nice person. Blonde, if it interests you. She doesn't look a bit like me. And if you think she's got anything to do with kidnapping girls and turning them into pornographic models you must be out of your mind!'

'But would I be so crazy to suspect you yourself, Mr Cousin?' Tansey asked quickly.

Cousin glared at him, and then shook his head sadly, as if the question were too stupid to demand a direct response. So Tansey continued to ask questions, and Cousin gave more or less satisfactory answers. Eventually the Chief Inspector decided that they had both had enough.

'Okay, Mr Cousin. I'll get a police car to take you home.'

'You mean I can go?' And when Tansey nodded, Peter Cousin added unexpectedly, 'You may not think so, Chief Inspector, but after what he did to Kate, I'd cheerfully kill this guy with my bare hands. I want him caught as much as you do. And I'm warning you he'll kill another of those girls soon, because she won't do as he asks, or because he's got bored with her body. You'd better find them quickly.'

CHAPTER 16

In retrospect Dick Tansey came to hope that he would never again have to live through a period like the next couple of days. Irrationally and incredibly, he found his imagination haunted by Peter Cousin's warning.

Tansey told himself repeatedly that the estate agent had merely been trying to get his own back for the indignity of being brought in for questioning by the police. Unless Cousin were indeed Browne his words must have been meaningless; there was no other conceivable way he could be certain that a second girl would be done away with. It was a guess on Cousin's part—a guess that was not unreasonable in the circumstances, Tansey admitted to himself—but a guess nevertheless.

But the Chief Inspector found it hard to shrug off the premonition—if that is what it was. Each time his phone rang, or each time Sergeant Greenway came into his room, her anxious green eyes belying her seemingly cold efficiency, he feared to learn what might have happened. And when Browne finally acted again, it was almost a relief.

John Seaton was fifteen; his brother, Hugh, a year younger. They were Scouts, and they had been brought up to be sensible, reliable and independent boys. The weather had suddenly changed, the rain giving way to a dry spell, and it was comparatively warm for the end of October in Oxford, so when John and Hugh said they planned to 'spend a night under canvas', their parents raised no violent objections, though they hinted that the garden of their house would be a good site for a camp.

The Seaton boys refused. They had camped in the garden before, and this time they intended to make sure that their mother didn't appear with hot drinks in the middle of a thunderstorm in their make-believe desert or jungle. Besides, they had found an excellent field that bordered on the Cherwell and was only a short distance from their home, so that it wouldn't be far to cart their gear. They set off after supper.

It was dark by then, but they had torches and a hurricane lamp, and they had made an efficient reconnaissance that same morning on their way to school. They put their tent up without difficulty in the shelter of a hedge, got into their sleeping-bags and made short work of the sandwiches and the contents of the Thermos flask that they had permitted their mother to provide.

They were warm, comfortable and rather pleased with themselves; the adventure would be something to mention casually at school the next day. Unfortunately, they were also a little bored. They had brought books, but the hurricane lamp threw dark shadows and it was an effort to hold the torches in the right position, so that reading was difficult. In the end, as there was nothing else to do, they decided to compose themselves for sleep.

Hugh, the younger boy, was the first to wake. He lay on his back and listened. There was a slithering noise, as if something was being dragged along the ground, then a grunt followed by a suppressed cough which reassured the youngster that it was not an animal. But who was it?

Gently Hugh woke his brother, and they both listened carefully. The sounds, which continued, came from the other side of the hedge. Clearly, whoever was there had a bad cold. There was no wind and the night was still so that, quite apart from his nagging cough, they could even hear his wheezy breathing.

'It could be a tramp,' John whispered.

Sitting up, he undid the flap of the tent and the boys peered out. At first they could see nothing. There was a fitful moon and one or two stars, often obscured by cloud, and at first it seemed very dark. Then gradually their eyes adjusted, though there was little to be seen through the narrow aperture in the tent. Filled with curiosity, they began to get up. It didn't occur to either of them to be afraid.

The tent was small. The sleeping-bags were side by side and it was almost impossible for the two young boys to wriggle out of them without making some noise. In the event John trod on Hugh's foot and Hugh gave a yelp of pain. And, any thought of caution now forgotten, they scrambled out of the tent and stood up.

From the other side of the hedge came what John later

described as 'a kind of roar of anger'. Then there was a loud splash, a smothered oath and the sound of someone running.

'We've frightened him,' Hugh said. 'He's made off.'

'He threw something in the river,' John said quickly. 'Come on, let's find it.' Then, 'Oh God! Look!'

For a moment the clouds had drifted off the moon and, as John pointed, the two boys saw a pale shape entangled in the roots of the briar that formed the edge of the hedge by the water. It was clearly a person, and already it was beginning to sink.

They had read about the missing girls, and the finding of Kate Minden's body in the river, and they had no doubt what they had just witnessed, so it says a great deal for their courage that they acted as they did. They ran to the bank, and John, flinging himself flat on the grass, just managed to make a long arm and get a grip on a shoulder before the body disappeared. With Hugh's help he pulled it up on to the bank.

They stared at each other, and John tentatively touched the naked form. It was icy, and it seemed to him to be quite dead.

'Quick!' he said to his brother. 'Get help—home's the nearest place you can be sure of anyone understanding at once. Get Father.'

As soon as his brother left, some memories of first aid instruction, together with a sense of innate modesty, made John hurry to the tent and bring their two sleeping-bags to wrap around the girl's nakedness. Then, shivering from reaction, he prepared to wait till help arrived.

Within an hour Chief Inspector Tansey was sitting on the Seatons' sofa, sipping a large brandy, and thankful that he was not one of the officers painstakingly searching the ground beside the river, now lit by floodlights. He had already been in touch with his Headquarters and the hospital to which the victim had been taken, and had issued certain strict instructions. Now the boys were drinking coffee, also laced with a little brandy, and he was listening to the details of their story with the greatest interest.

'You did splendidly, both of you,' he said, 'and your mates will be asking you lots of questions when you go back to school—not this morning, I suggest,' he interpolated, glancing at the parents—'but perhaps tomorrow. When you do meet your friends there are one or two things it's terribly important for you to remember. Make sure you understand what I'm saying.'

The boys nodded in unison, and Tansey went on, 'First, you must say firmly that you did not see the man on the other side of the hedge. You never even got a glimpse of him.'

'That's true,' John said. 'We didn't.'

'Well, keep it like that,' his father ordered. 'Don't try to embroider the story. This chap is a murdering psychopath. You know what that means?'

'He's barmy,' Hugh said.

'And he's dangerous! If he thought you'd seen him and might remember something distinctive about him, he could decide to come after you.'

This was not all that Tansey had in mind; personally, he did not believe the young Seatons were in any danger. But he was very fearful for the two girls whom Browne still held. If Browne were to suspect, however erroneously, that the police were close to identifying him because of what had happened that night, he might panic and kill them both.

'The second point is equally important,' said Tansey. 'You must not suggest in any way—you must not give the merest hint to anyone—that the girl you pulled out of the river might be alive.'

'She—I didn't realize she was, until she suddenly sort of burped.' John Seaton grimaced. 'I know it was stupid, but it scared me stiff for a moment. But it made me remember my Scout training; I knew what I ought to be doing.'

'So you started the "kiss of life",' Tansey said gently. 'And if she lives, it'll be thanks to you.'

'She was beautiful,' John said suddenly and, to his annoyance and his parents' obvious amusement, he blushed scarlet. 'But we won't forget, sir. We'll be careful what we say —at school and to any reporters.' He hurried on. 'As far as we're concerned, the lady was dead, a body. That makes a grim enough story, anyway.'

'Yes, indeed.' Regretfully the Chief Inspector finished his drink, and refused another. 'I must be off. Thank you for your help. I'll leave a man around the house,' he added to Mr Seaton. 'The boy's right about reporters; they'll do their best to catch them—and catch them out. Perhaps it would be best to keep them home till the weekend.'

Tansey next paid a brief visit to the inspector who was coordinating the efforts of the officers in the field beside the river. They had found a shoe print which might be relevant, and had covered it carefully until a cast could be taken in daylight. Otherwise, they had so far had no luck.

The Chief Inspector left them to their task, and drove to the hospital, where he was immediately accosted by a white-faced Paul Avery.

'What's happened, Chief Inspector? Where did you find Linda? It was just chance I was on duty, and a colleague told me she'd been brought in. Was acid used on her? My God, the least you could have done was let me know. She *is* my wife! Why didn't you?'

'Because I've been too busy, Dr Avery,' Tansey said icily, 'and because I gave strict orders that she was to be brought here quite anonymously and in secret. Your colleague was at fault in releasing her name, and I sincerely hope you haven't told anyone else. Do you know how she is?'

Avery looked slightly abashed. 'No, I don't. They won't let me near her. I suppose that's the result of your instructions, too. But I know she's in a room next to intensive care, and there was talk of a life-support machine.' Avery gestured hopelessly. 'I know your Sergeant Greenway's with her, too. She was allowed in,' he added bitterly. 'For God's sake, Tansey! What the hell's going on?'

Tansey stared at Avery, and relented. 'It's all right, Doctor,' he said. 'There's no question of acid, and there are good reasons for the orders I've given. I just hope they've been obeyed. Now, you get us some coffee, and I'll find out exactly what's happening.'

A nurse, who had been standing by in silence during this interchange, took Tansey to Linda Jackson's room and brought Hilary Greenway out to him. The Sergeant was pale, and there were dark circles under her eyes.

'She's still alive,' Greenway said. 'Just. But I don't think there's much hope, sir, from what I can gather. Her heart stopped, but they got it working again, and they say she's stable now. I think that's just a word they use when they don't know what to say. As far as I can tell, she's unconscious —in a coma.'

'Poor girl—and poor Dr Avery,' said Tansey with real sympathy. Then suddenly his anger erupted. 'Why the hell did that bastard Browne have to try to kill her? She hadn't been marked with acid. The Seaton boy who pulled her out said she was beautiful. I don't understand it. Did Browne merely get tired of her? And what about her hair?'

'She wasn't shaved, sir, if that's what you're thinking. Her hair had just been cut very short, quickly and roughly.'

'And why's she so ill? She's not still half-drowned, surely?'

'No, sir. It's drugs—they're trying to discover the exact kind. One of the doctors suggested she might have tried to kill herself.'

'What?'

'As you said, sir, she was unmarked, but she may well have known about Kate. She may even have seen it happen, and decided there was no hope she'd ever get out alive. So she somehow managed to take an overdose of the sedative

Browne and company are feeding the girls to keep them quiet and acquiescent. Alternatively, she might simply have refused to cooperate any more, whatever the threats, and been given an overdose.'

Tansey nodded gloomily. 'Browne must have known she was alive when he put her into the water,' he said. 'I suppose he intended to hold her under, but the boys interrupted him. He must be worried sick at the moment in case Linda's telling us all. I hope to Christ we can conceal the fact that she's alive, so that the media'll reassure him quickly. We don't want him panicking and killing Rust and Sinclair at this stage. I've had a word with the chief administrator here, and he's warned the staff, I know. Though there's been one leak—to her husband—but I think I caught it in time.'

The Rusts would have to be told it was Linda Jackson, Tansey realized—and Bill Sinclair, before they learnt from the media that a second girl had been pulled from the water. But they could be left to believe her dead—unlike Linda's parents, who must be told the truth. Had Avery let them know? Were they already on their way? He'd need Greenway beside him to help with all this, Tansey reflected. Someone else would have to sit by Linda in case she regained consciousness and said something vital.

Sergeant Greenway seemed to be reading his thoughts. 'I've already sent for WPC Campbell, sir, and she's here. Not that the medical people hold out much hope that Linda will come round, as I said, but—'

'You mean there's no encouragement we can offer poor Avery? He's meant to be fetching coffee. All I've told him so far is that acid wasn't used. I'll have to put him in the full picture,' Tansey went on. 'His mere presence here and his obvious anxiety could give the game away.'

'We can tell him she was heavily drugged and her lovely hair was cut short, but she hasn't been physically or sexually abused or—or hurt as Kate was. We can even say we're told she's stable, though I doubt if that'll be much consolation to him. But after all, she's not dead yet, sir. She's young and healthy, and she's got everything to fight for.'

Tansey grinned. 'You go and have coffee with Dr Avery, Sergeant. You'll be far better for him than I will. Confirm that Linda's parents have been informed, and make sure they—and the doctor—understand the situation and the need for secrecy. As I've said before, I hope to God we can keep the fact that she's alive quiet. It's a pretty forlorn hope by this time, I suppose, but we must try. Anyway, do your best. Then meet me at Headquarters. All right?'

'Yes, sir.' She returned his smile.

The Chief Inspector nodded and hurried away. There was a lot to be done by morning, before most people went to work. Neither he nor Sergeant Greenway was going to get any more sleep that night.

Shortly before 9.00 a.m. Tansey went along to the officers' canteen. He was bleary-eyed, but he had washed and shaved and was wearing the clean shirt he always kept in his desk drawer for emergencies such as this. He ordered black coffee, eggs and bacon, and took them to a small table by the window wall. It was an unwritten rule of the mess that if an officer wanted to join his colleagues in conversation he was welcome, but if he wanted to be alone no one would take offence. This morning Tansey wanted to be alone.

He needed to think. As he ate his breakfast and felt the reviving warmth of the coffee he reviewed what he had accomplished during the last few hours, mentally ticking off each item to make sure nothing had been forgotten. There still remained a full report to be prepared, and a check must be made on the results of the search of the field by the river. And he must phone the hospital, though he knew he would have been informed if there had been any great change in Linda Jackson's condition.

Then what? He had listened to the local radio station carefully, and noted with satisfaction the newscaster's

categorical statement that Linda had been dead when she
was pulled out of the water. He hoped that Browne had
heard the statement too, and that no later bulletins would
contradict it.

But what would Browne do now? He could kill Mary Rust
and Jane Sinclair and, with the help of his companion,
dump their bodies somewhere. Then, if he took no further
action, and Linda Jackson failed to regain consciousness,
he might never be traced—until the urge to defile another
beautiful girl seized him, which might not be for months, or
even years.

But somehow Tansey didn't believe this. Browne had been
growing bolder; his attack on Jane Sinclair, though carefully
prepared, had bordered on rashness. The fright he had received last night when he was disposing of Linda might deter
him temporarily, but not, Tansey was inclined to think, for
long. Once he was sure that Linda had been able to do him
no harm, he would continue. He still had two models on his
hands, and how was he to be prevented from seizing a third
—a substitute for Linda? Aware that Browne was still at least
one step ahead of him, the Chief Inspector could think of no
immediate answer to his questions.

CHAPTER 17

The telephone was ringing as Tansey reached his office and,
suddenly sure that it was the hospital with news of Linda
Jackson, he almost flung himself around his desk to reach
the instrument before it stopped. But his premonition had
been quite wrong; it was not the hospital on the line.
Surprisingly, the call was from Quentin Wood.

'Chief Inspector, are you still interested in that photograph of my granddaughter with the ribbon round her
waist?'

It was the last question that Tansey had expected. 'Yes,' he said carefully. 'I am. Why do you ask?'

'Because I've just remembered where my—my inspiration, shall we call it?—came from. I was looking through an old album last night when it hit me. Juxtaposition of ideas, I suppose, or something like that.'

'Yes, Mr Wood. But what was it that hit you?' Tansey asked patiently.

'Well, as you know, I'd come to flatter myself that as I was watching the child play with the ribbon I'd had a brilliantly original idea but, as one might have expected, it wasn't so at all. What had happened was that I'd seen a very similar photograph before, ages ago, and it must have stuck in my memory.'

'Do you remember where? Where you saw the original, I mean?' By now Tansey was acutely interested.

'In a shop window, in Reading. I was so intrigued by it that I went and asked if they would sell me a print.'

'And did they?'

'Oh yes. That's the point. I think I may still have it somewhere.'

'Do you remember the name of the shop?'

'No, but it may be on the back of the print. If you're really interested I could probably find it. It will mean grubbing through a lot of boxes of old photos, and will take time, which is why I'm checking with you first. It's not a task I'd undertake for fun, I assure you.'

'Mr Wood, to be candid, I can't promise you that it will be in the least useful,' Tansey said earnestly. 'You may be wasting your time, and mine. But it might break the case wide open. So please do your best, and let me know as soon as you can. We shall be very grateful.'

Tansey put down his receiver thoughtfully. It was perhaps an odd coincidence that Wood's memory should have been jogged at about the same time that Browne was planning to dispose of Linda Jackson, but coincidences did happen.

And, if Wood were telling the truth, it could just possibly represent an important lead to Browne. It was a long shot, but they were reduced to long shots. And unfortunately, thought Tansey, it didn't necessarily eliminate Wood himself.

By 11.00 a.m. the Chief Inspector had acquired a few more facts. It was blood on the back of the last batch of slides —and blood of the relatively uncommon group A. The sole-print found in the field by the river had turned out to be of a shoe of a well-known brand, size eight, and with no obvious distinguishing marks; there was however nothing to connect it directly with the incident, except that it had been close beside marks which suggested that Linda Jackson had been dragged part of the way in a sack or a large laundry bag.

The best news was that Linda herself was showing signs of emerging from her coma. She had muttered once or twice; the sounds she had made were unintelligible but Paul Avery, who had finally been permitted to see her, was full of hope. The consultant in charge was less optimistic, and Tansey deliberately suppressed his own feelings of delight.

At 11.15 Quentin Wood was once more on the phone. 'I've found that print,' he said. 'Absolute luck. What shall I do with it? I don't think it's going to be a great help. It's merely stamped, "Vic. Reading" on the back.'

'I'll send someone to collect it right away,' Tansey said. 'Thank you very much.'

'Send that sergeant with the nice legs,' Wood said, and laughed.

Tansey repeated the remark, and said, 'You'd better be careful, Sergeant Greenway.'

'I'm always careful, sir,' she replied, 'but luckily I don't have long hair, so I should be safe.'

Thankful for a moment's light relief, Dick Tansey grinned. 'I'll be waiting outside in the car, anyway. Then we'll go straight to Reading. It may be a wild goose chase, but if there's anything in it we could save a lot of time by going ourselves.'

'Very good, sir.'

'And when you collect the photo have a look at Wood's feet, Sergeant, while he's inspecting your legs.'

'His feet? Yes, sir. Shall I ask him what his blood group is, too?'

'No. Leave that for now,' Tansey said.

But a half-hour later when Sergeant Greenway returned to the car and handed Tansey the print that Wood had given her, she said, 'Quentin Wood's feet are long and rather elegant. Size eleven, I would guess. He was wearing calf shoes, well-worn but hand-made, probably to his own last. That print in the field was certainly not his.' She paused and started the engine. 'His blood group, however, is A.'

'I thought I said—' Tansey began.

'I didn't ask him, sir,' Greenway said quickly. 'But the housekeeper left me in his study while she went to fetch him. He was in what she called the "photo department" in the basement. One of those slim leather diaries that people carry about with them was lying on his desk, and I glanced inside. Among the "Personal Notes", between his national insurance number and his passport number, was his blood group.'

'Well done,' said Tansey. 'I suppose that could help. Incidentally, I phoned Mr Knight while you were in Wood's house. I thought he might have records of his staff—for insurance purposes, say—and it turns out that Peter Cousin is also group A.'

'A pity,' Greenway said. She sighed. 'You can laugh at my female intuition if you like, sir, but I do not believe that Cousin's our man.'

In Reading they made their way straight to the main police station to inquire about photographic studios. There were at least six in the downtown area, they were informed, not to speak of a wide variety of others in the suburbs of the city, where studios were more often a sideline in shops which sold photographic equipment. A trade directory disclosed that none of them was called Vic. When Tansey persisted, an elderly sergeant, who was working out his time until he became due for his full pension, was produced. He supported his colleagues.

'I've been here for thirty years, sir,' he said, 'and I don't remember there was ever a photographer's called Vic. But it might be he is—or was—an employee, and was allowed to put his name on some of his photos. It's not usual, perhaps, but I can't see any reason why it shouldn't be done, if a studio gets hold of a good chap, say, and wants to keep him.'

Tansey thanked him. He had hoped for better luck, but it was clear that every studio would have to be visited. However, with some difficulty he arranged for the suburban establishments to be visited by local officers while he and Sergeant Greenway divided the ones in the centre of the city. By the time they met for a late lunch, they knew their own calls had been wasted effort; no one in the downtown area had ever heard of a photographer called Vic.

The reports from the suburbs were equally depressing. Then the elderly sergeant pointed out that about a year ago there had been a bad fire at a photographer's shop in one of the outer suburbs of the city. It was called Stein's, he recalled, and had a good local reputation. The owner, David Stein, had been killed in the fire, and his wife had left the area, as far as he knew.

As a last resort therefore, shortly after 3.00 that afternoon Tansey and Greenway found themselves staring at a derelict, burnt-out building. The Chief Inspector finally exploded. 'This is a bloody stupid game,' he said angrily. 'We're achieving absolutely nothing, and God knows what's happening at Headquarters.'

'It's not long since I called in, sir,' said Greenway
soothingly. 'And now we're here, mightn't it be worth
a try? We could ask around at one or two of the neigh-
bouring shops? They may well know something about the
business that was there. It would be surprising if they
didn't.'

Reluctantly Tansey agreed, knowing that Greenway was
right. 'Okay, Sergeant,' he said. 'I'll check with HQ again,
and you see what you can do.'

'Yes, sir. I shan't take long.'

He watched her walk briskly along the street and disap-
pear into a beauty parlour. His thoughts wandered. He
brought them back sharply to duty and reality, and called
up Kidlington. There was nothing new, except for an extraordinary statement from Mr Rust that he hoped his daughter, Mary, was dead, because after the dreadful things she
had done he and his wife could never welcome her into their
home again.

Tansey was still seething with anger on Mary Rust's
behalf when the sergeant put her head in the car window.
Her eyes were bright with excitement as she said, 'Sir, I
think you should come and speak to a Mrs Wadham. She's
the lady who runs the beauty salon there, and she knew
the Steins well when they had their photographic business
almost next door.'

'Vic?' Tansey asked as he walked beside her towards the
beauty salon.

'I hope so, sir, but let her tell you.'

Mrs Wadham was a woman in her late forties. She was
short, plump, pretty, heavily made up and heavily scented,
with extraordinarily long nails—presumably advertising the
prowess of her manicurist—on her many-ringed hands.
Though it was mid-afternoon, she wore a low-cut, black
taffeta dress which would have been more suitable for a
cocktail party. She had been friendly to Sergeant Greenway,
but she positively dazzled the Chief Inspector with her

smiles. Tansey, somewhat overwhelmed, did his best to respond.

'If you could spare the time to answer a few questions, madam, we should be extremely grateful.'

'Of course, Chief Inspector. Come along into my office. I'll get one of my girls to bring us some tea. Or would you prefer coffee? Or something stronger?'

'Tea would be splendid, thank you,' said Tansey politely, careful not to exchange glances with Greenway.

Mrs Wadham led the way to a small room towards the rear of the premises. It was furnished practically and austerely, in contrast to its owner but, as she seated herself behind her desk, there was no doubt about Mrs Wadham's acuity or authority. Tea arrived almost at once, and it was not until she had poured and passed cups and a plate of chocolate biscuits that she allowed the conversation to get down to business.

Then she said, 'Now, what exactly do you want to know about the poor Steins?'

'We're trying to trace a photographer called Vic, who's wanted as a witness in a case,' Tansey explained. 'I gather that Vic worked for the Steins.'

'Yes, for about two years. And I can tell you it made a tremendous difference to their business. David Stein was a dear man, but he was in his sixties and he was set in his ways. You know, the standard set of wedding prints. The young want more than that these days—sometimes I think they're going back to Victorian times, with haloes around their faces and imaginary romantic settings. And Vic had flair, tremendous flair; there was no doubt about it. You could say that Stein's was transformed. From being a rather pathetic second-rate sort of establishment, it became first class of its kind, with a booming business. Mind you, I'm not saying Vic was a second Karsh or Snowdon, but a photograph by Vic was guaranteed to be original and interesting.'

Tansey produced from his wallet the print of the baby with the bow that Quentin Wood had found for them. 'Do you recognize this?' he asked.

'Yes, indeed.' Without hesitation Mrs Wadham nodded her head vigorously. 'Stein had it on display in the middle of his shop window for ages. He said he thought it was a work of genius.' She handed back the photograph, and sighed gustily. 'Poor David. Poor Marie. So very sad.'

'Tell us about it. What happened?' Tansey prompted when Mrs Wadham bit into a chocolate biscuit and seemed to have reached the end of her story.

'I told your colleague here,' Mrs Wadham remarked, 'but I don't mind repeating it for you. Everything suddenly went wrong. Vic left the Steins. Don't ask me why, because I don't know. Marie wouldn't tell me. All she'd say was that there had been a misunderstanding about something, that David hadn't been very tactful and Vic had been offended. Anyway, Vic went—I've no idea where—and the business subsided into what it had been before. Then there was the fire.'

'When did all this happen, Mrs Wadham?'

'Vic left sometime last autumn, Chief Inspector. I can't remember exactly when. And the fire was shortly before Christmas. The firemen were splendid. They managed to stop it spreading to the other houses in the row—including this one—though heaven knows how. The studio was completely gutted, as you can see for yourselves. I do wish someone would come along and rebuild. It's bad for the neighbourhood—and bad for business—having a derelict place like that on the doorstep.'

'What about Mr and Mrs Stein? He died in the fire, I gather.'

'They both got out, but David went back to fetch something and was overcome by smoke. They found his body later. As for poor Marie, the shock affected her mind. She was in hospital for months. I went to visit her once or twice. She'd aged twenty years, and scarcely seemed to know who I was.'

'Is she still in hospital?'

'No. She's living with her married daughter, a Mrs Mercer. I have the address. It's in a place called Colombury, in the Cotswolds. I promised to keep in touch.'

'Colombury!' exclaimed Tansey in surprise.

'Why? Do you know it?'

'Oh yes, we know it,' said Tansey briefly.

Mrs Wadham stared at him for a moment, then said, 'Well, I doubt if Marie'll be able to help you trace Vic, Colombury or no Colombury.'

'We can but try,' Tansey said, and wondered how often he had used those banal words.

While Mrs Wadham dictated the address to Sergeant Greenway he thought about Vic, the brilliant photographer. The chances were that he had nothing whatever to do with Browne's pornography. If the baby with the bow had been in Stein's window for weeks, even months, many people could have been attracted by it, just like Quentin Wood, and Browne could have been one of them. Nevertheless, the lead must be followed up.

'Thank you, Mrs Wadham. Thank you very much indeed. With that information, we should be able to find Mrs Stein easily,' said Greenway as she finished writing. 'Incidentally, what was Vic's surname?'

Mrs Wadham looked at the sergeant through her wide, mascaraed eyes. 'You know, it's absurd, but I've no idea. Marie and David always spoke of Vic as Vic and nothing else. But Marie might be able to tell you.'

'I expect so,' said Tansey, more cheerfully than he felt. Vic was beginning to sound increasingly elusive. 'Anyway, we're very grateful to you for all your help, Mrs Wadham, and for the tea. Now we must go, and not keep you any longer. I suppose you wouldn't know where Vic lived in

Reading? The landlady might have been left a forwarding address.'

'No. I'm sorry. I think she lived with a friend, but I don't know who or where.'

'Did you say *she*?' Tansey was stunned.

'Yes, of course.' Mrs Wadham laughed. 'How funny! You thought Vic was a man. No, it must have been short for Victoria, say, rather than Victor. Vic was certainly a woman, though not an attractive one. She had big hands and feet, and a big nose. I don't think any man would ever have looked at her twice, even when she was young— and she's gone fifty now—but she did take marvellous pictures.'

'Yes,' said Tansey weakly. 'Well, thank you once again, Mrs Wadham.'

CHAPTER 18

'A woman!' Greenway said. 'I—I can't believe it, sir. I was so sure Vic was going to turn out to be Browne.'

'I had hopes, too,' Tansey admitted. 'As it is, we might as well face the fact that there's probably no connection between Browne and Vic. All that happened was that both Browne and Quentin Wood saw Vic's photograph of that baby and were impressed by it.' The Chief Inspector restrained his frustration to a single, 'Damn!'

He and Sergeant Greenway had left Reading, and were driving north and west to the rolling Cotswold hills and the market town of Colombury. Tansey had used the car radio to trace Mrs Mercer's number, and get himself patched through to it. He explained their mission and, after some initial hesitation, the daughter had assured him that her mother, Mrs Stein, was 'having a good day', and would be happy to talk to them.

'But she lives in the past now,' Mrs Mercer had warned, 'and you can't rely on her memory. It comes and goes. Anyway, I'm sure she'll do her best to help you. And please do try not to trouble or upset her.'

Tansey promised to be at his most tactful, and Hilary Greenway drove steadily towards Colombury. She was a good driver, and enjoyed driving, but it had been a very long day. And at the end, what? she thought. In all likelihood, Vic —Victoria Noname—if they ever found her, would turn out to be an unattractive, vaguely unhappy woman with imagination and a flair for photography, who would have been appalled by the obscenity of *Beautiful Butterflies*, if she had ever chanced to see the magazine. Nevertheless, she would have used up a considerable amount of Dick Tansey's time and energy, which he could ill afford if he were to succeed in bringing the case to a successful conclusion in a reasonable time.

For a moment Sergeant Greenway took her eyes off the road to glance at Tansey, but he was gazing out of his window, his face expressionless. She would have been surprised to know that he was thinking, not of Browne or the two girls still held captive, not of Linda Jackson or Vic, not even of their latest surprising discovery, but of his sergeant, sitting next to him.

They were on the outskirts of Colombury when Tansey came to life and said, 'We go right through the town, along that hideous bit of ribbon development, and take the left fork at the Y-junction. There's a row of council houses opposite some wooded land. We want the first one.'

Greenway followed his instructions, and pulled up in front of a neat box-like house. 'At least there's no parking problem here,' she said as she unlatched the low gate and stood back to let the Chief Inspector precede her up the narrow garden path.

Their arrival at the front door was anticipated. Before Tansey could ring it was opened by a small, dark woman, who greeted them with a nervous, worried expression. This was Mrs Mercer. Tansey introduced himself and Sergeant Greenway.

'I've spoken to Mother and she'll tell you anything she can,' said Mrs Mercer, 'but I do hope this doesn't mean more trouble for her. She's had enough recently, one way and another.'

'I appreciate that,' Tansey said soothingly, 'and we've no intention of causing her any trouble. We just want to ask her about an assistant, called Vic, whom Mr Stein employed at his studio.'

'I know, you said. Vic—yes, well,' Mrs Mercer didn't sound reassured. 'As long as you realize that Mother gets strange ideas in her head, you can't really rely on what she says.'

'I understand, Mrs Mercer,' Tansey said. 'Please don't worry.'

Mrs Mercer shrugged at what she clearly considered a stupid admonition, but she showed them into the front room where Mrs Stein, a larger, fatter version of her daughter, sat in an armchair, with her swollen ankles supported by a stool. She was watching television and objected somewhat resentfully when the set was turned off, but became reconciled after a little flattery from the Chief Inspector.

'Yes, of course I'll tell you what I know about Vic, but it isn't much—and it brings back unhappy memories.' Mrs Stein took a small handkerchief from the sleeve of her jumper and, in what was intended as a token gesture, blew her nose. 'Vic was a strange woman. Not friendly,' she went on. 'She kept herself to herself. I never liked her much, to tell the truth, even before the fire.'

'Now, Mother,' Mrs Mercer said warningly.

Mrs Stein glared at her daughter. 'Well, it's true, isn't it? Why shouldn't I tell this nice policeman the truth?'

When Mrs Mercer produced no answer to this Tansey said, 'What was Vic's last name, Mrs Stein?'

'Vic's last name?' There was a long pause while Mrs Stein thought. 'You know, I can't remember. She was Miss—She wasn't married. No one would have married her. She was an ugly woman. Miss—Miss Something. It was a short name. One syllable. But no. I can't remember.'

'Do you know, Mrs Mercer?' Tansey asked.

'No. I've no idea. I never met the woman, and the matter never came up. Mother always referred to her as Vic.'

'Her name couldn't have been Browne, could it?'

'No,' said Mrs Stein firmly. 'It wasn't Brown or Green or Grey or any colour. Of that I'm sure.'

Tansey gave up, and changed the subject. 'Have you any idea where she went when she left you, Mrs Stein?'

'Back to London where she came from, I suppose,' said Mrs Stein. 'Father had put an advertisement in the local paper, and she turned up in answer to it. She said she came from London, and she'd had some experience. It wasn't easy to find someone responsible, and Father could tell from the way she spoke that she knew about photography, so he took her on. He was right, too. I'll say that for her. She was wonderful at the job.'

'She had no references?'

'I don't think so. If she did they'd have been lost in the fire, like everything else.' Mrs Stein became sunk in gloom.

Tansey tried to rouse her by asking more questions, but he learnt little from her answers. Vic didn't run a car, though she might have known how to drive; she came to work by bus or on foot. She said she lived in a small flat with a friend, but the Steins had never been asked there. What was more, Vic had always refused social invitations from the Steins, and they'd never met the friend. Apart from a cold Vic had never been ill and, as far as Mrs Stein knew, had never gone to a doctor or a dentist in Reading.

Dick Tansey paused in his questioning. He was getting nowhere, he realized. There was no doubt that, given time, the elusive Vic could be traced through the authorities—

inland revenue, national insurance and so on. But the lack
of detail, the fire and the destruction of Mr Stein's own
business records would make this a long job. The attempt
would have to be made, of course, but they must hope for
a short cut. Those girls' lives were only safe, and the possibility of an arrest only existed, while Browne thought that
Linda Jackson was dead. Once stories began to get around—

He saw Sergeant Greenway swallow a yawn, and he
sympathized. They still had to drive back to Kidlington,
and he would have paperwork waiting for him there. He
was tempted to leave it at that, to thank Mrs Stein, and go.

Then she said, 'Why do you want to find Vic, Chief
Inspector? Has she burnt down someone else's house?'

'Mother!' Mrs Mercer protested. 'You mustn't say things
like that, suggesting that Vic . . . It's slander, and it's not
true! Vic left the shop weeks before the fire, Chief Inspector.
The police said they supposed it could have been arson, but
there was no indication of it—and certainly no proof, and
there was no reason on earth why poor Vic—'

'Poor Vic!' repeated her mother scathingly. 'And, oh yes,
there was a reason. But I was ill at the time, in hospital,
after the fire, Chief Inspector. It was only later I could bring
myself to think about it, and I remembered how Vic had
looked. If looks could kill, she'd have killed David there and
then. He thought it was a joke, and he laughed. But to
her—'

'Mother doesn't know what she's talking about, Chief
Inspector,' Mrs Mercer said quickly. 'I told you she gets
muddled and—'

'I'm not in the least muddled!' Mrs Stein contradicted
her daughter obstinately and emphatically. 'I can't prove
it. The police can't prove it. No one can prove it. But, as
sure as I'm alive now after that ghastly fire, it was Vic—'
She stopped and stared helplessly at Tansey. 'I nearly got
her last name then,' she said, puzzled.

'I warned you, Chief Inspector.' Mrs Mercer seized her

opportunity again. 'Mother means well, but her mind isn't what it was. It wanders, and she gets confused.'

'Yes, of course.' Tansey uttered meaningless words which he hoped would reassure both women. 'There's one thing you haven't told us,' he continued, smiling at them, 'and that's why Vic left, when she was doing so well as a photographer. It obviously wasn't anything to do with her work.'

'It was because Father offended her.' Mrs Stein had recovered her wits. 'I wasn't there when it happened, but he told me all about it. It was just an accident. He fell over a tripod or a cable or something and—Normally he'd never have laid a hand on her, but if you're falling you clutch at whatever's nearest, and on this occasion it was Vic's head. So silly. But Father had no idea. It was a shock to him. And he laughed. That's when I came in and I saw her face. She was uglier than ever.'

'He laughed?' Tansey tried to fill the gap of incomprehension that had followed Mrs Stein's last words. 'Why, Mrs Stein? Why did he laugh?'

She shrugged. 'Nervous reaction, perhaps. Father was a nervy man. And embarrassment, I dare say. He said to me afterwards her pate was so smooth it reminded him of a baby's bottom, and he could have stroked it. She was wearing a wig, of all things—a wig. But he wasn't laughing *at* Vic, though he couldn't make her understand that. She was very angry. She never forgave him—or me. She gave in her notice the next day, and was gone within the week. But she came back. I don't care what anyone says. Vic came back and set fire to the studio and—and killed my David.'

Mrs Stein burst into tears. This time her little handkerchief was totally inadequate, and her daughter went to her aid, murmuring consoling phrases. Tansey and Greenway exchanged glances. Each knew what the other was thinking, that at the end of the day they had struck gold.

'I'm sorry,' Mrs Mercer said, 'but I'll have to ask you to go now. Mother's upset, and you won't get any more out of her until she's taken her pills and had a good night's sleep.'

There was no option. Tansey apologized as Mrs Mercer saw them to the door. Mrs Stein had stopped crying, and was staring at the blank screen of the television set.

'Please,' Tansey said in the hall. 'If your mother recalls Vic's second name, or anything else that would help us to identify her, will you let us know at once. It could be terribly important. If you'd phone that number.' He passed her his card.

Mrs Mercer accepted it without enthusiasm. 'Why do you want to find this Vic so much?' she asked. 'She can't have had anything to do with the fire, in spite of what Mother says. I told you, she'd gone weeks before it happened.'

'She's wanted as a witness in a very important case,' Tansey replied, repeating the half-lie he had told Mrs Wadham earlier.

Mrs Mercer seemed to miss the point. 'Mother wouldn't be any good as a witness. She doesn't know what she's saying most of the time. She makes things up. You mustn't trust her, Chief Inspector.'

They were out of Colombury town before Tansey spoke. 'I wouldn't want to put the old girl on the stand, but I believed her. Didn't you, Sergeant?'

'Yes,' said Greenway without hesitation. 'She certainly didn't make up that bit about her husband pulling off Vic's wig by accident, and Vic being furious. In the circumstances of this case, it would be too great a coincidence that once we'd found an expert photographer who had taken that baby picture, his employer's wife should invent a story about hair—or lack of it.'

Tansey grunted his agreement. 'I'm not so sure about the fire, and maybe that doesn't matter, though it was very convenient for Vic that Stein's records were all destroyed. What does matter is that Browne—or Vic as we now know her—is no longer an amorphous figure. She's got a past and, by God, I hope to arrange her future.'

'There's one thing that worries me about her, sir,' Greenway said tentatively.'

'Yes?' Tansey yawned involuntarily.

'She's apparently a singularly unattractive woman. Mrs Stein, who's no beauty, called her ugly, and Mrs Wadham said no man would ever look at her twice,' Greenway said thoughtfully, weighing her words. 'Yet some man is prepared to help her abduct girls, take obscene pictures of them and—and kill for her sake. I know he didn't actually kill Kate, but he did his best with Linda, and we're pretty sure he strangled Gus Hunter. It strikes me as odd, sir—a contradiction.'

Tansey was shaking his head. 'I'm not sure it's quite like that, Sergeant.' For several miles he said no more. He had suddenly seen how it could have been, how it almost certainly was, and with infinite care he was checking the case in his mind to ensure that there were no great barriers to his new theory. When he could find none, he said at last, 'I'm not convinced that there *is* a man involved. I think we've been looking for a character who doesn't exist.'

'But—but we *know* there are two of them, sir,' Greenway objected. 'Apart from anything else, there was that boy who saw them together in the Ford Escort in Abingdon when Jane Sinclair was seized, and—'

'Two persons, yes, Sergeant,' Tansey agreed. 'But we've no firm evidence to prove that one was a man. On the contrary it makes more sense if they were both women. We've always said Kate Minden was too sensible to accept a lift from a strange man, but if two not-so-young ladies ask her the way to Abingdon, and when she says that's where she's going, offer her a place in their car—Well, wouldn't you have jumped at it?'

'Yes, I suppose I would,' Greenway admitted. 'That would apply to Mary Rust, too, wouldn't it? Running away from her Brian she'd have felt safe with any women. But

Linda Jackson was too close to home to take a lift from anyone, and Jane Sinclair, we know, was taken by force. And there's Gus Hunter to be accounted for, too.'

'Remember, Hunter was a small man, and he was knocked out before he was strangled. And all the girls were slightly built. Whereas Vic's been described as tallish, with large hands and feet, and ugly—in fact, a masculine type female. Of course, it'll all need checking. Her voice, too, Was it deep? Could she have convinced the Ewans on the phone that she was a man?' The Chief Inspector was now thinking aloud. 'We know she lived with a "friend" in Reading. This could be the one with the woolly cap, the more female half of the relationship, perhaps.'

Sergeant Greenway shuddered. 'Sorry, sir, but—but if you're right it makes the whole thing far worse. I find it hard to conceive that women should do these dreadful things to—to their own. When I think of Kate—'

'I know,' said Tansey softly. 'I know. But sometimes that's the way the world is. And at least we seem to be getting somewhere at last.'

CHAPTER 19

'No,' said the Chief Constable. 'I'm sorry, but I really don't think it's on. There must be hundreds of women in the district living in pairs, women of all ages, perfectly well-meaning respectable women, who would be as shocked by these pornographic pictures as—as your own mother would be.'

'My mother is dead, sir,' Tansey said coldly, aware that this didn't affect the argument.

Philip Midvale rightly ignored the remark. 'So why pick on them?' he demanded.

'They fit such descriptions as we have. They own a car

of the right make and year and colour. I should have spotted
the name when I went through the computer print-out from
the motor licensing bureau; that was one mistake I made,
sir,' Tansey admitted. 'And Linda Jackson—'

'Could easily have been seized and bundled into a car by
force, as the Sinclair girl was,' Midvale interrupted. 'In fact,
it would have been a far safer operation. I would hazard
that the chances of someone turning into the alley at the
time Sinclair was attacked were vastly greater than someone
chancing on Jackson's abduction in that dark residential
crescent in the evening.'

The Chief Inspector didn't agree with this, given the
circumstances at the time of the Sinclair attack, but he
didn't argue. He said, 'They have a large detached house,
sir, with attics and an attached garage, which would be
useful.'

'For carrying shopping directly into the kitchen, perhaps.'
Philip Midvale was not usually sarcastic. 'So do a great
many other people in North Oxford, Chief Inspector—'

'Sir—' interrupted Tansey.

'No,' said the Chief Constable. 'Let me finish. What
you've done is form an hypothesis—a theory—then try to
collect or interpret facts to prove it. As far as I'm concerned,
you haven't found enough facts. For instance, you've no
reason to believe that either of these ladies knows one end
of a camera from another. I see your point about Linda
Jackson, and the danger of the story getting around that
she's alive, but I still don't think it justifies what you're
suggesting.'

Tansey opened his mouth to comment further. In the first
place it was basic to his argument that one of the ladies was
Vic. Secondly, he could try once again to emphasize the
potential danger of delay. Then he shut it again. The Chief
Constable had decided; it was useless to discuss the matter.

Of course there was a reason for the Chief Constable's
attitude, reflected Tansey. The media had not been kind to

the Thames Valley Police Force recently and Midvale, who always supported his officers in public, had borne the brunt of the criticism. Tansey appreciated this, but he also felt strongly that his request was justified. He hesitated.

'So you're ordering me not to apply for a search warrant, sir?' he said at length.

'Yes, that's just what I'm doing. Think what the media will make of it if you search the house of two middle-aged women and find absolutely nothing to connect them with these crimes. We'd be a laughing-stock.'

'Supposing we found Rust and Sinclair up in the attics, sir,' Tansey couldn't resist saying.

'And suppose we didn't?'

'Suppose—' Tansey began, and stopped. The conversation was rapidly becoming one of those 'Yes, you did; no, I didn't' dialogues. 'Very good, sir,' he said. 'But I may continue with this line of investigation?'

'If you think it necessary, of course. But be tactful about it, Chief Inspector, for God's sake.'

'I shall certainly do my best, sir,' Tansey said, and thought that was a promise he would make every effort to keep—because otherwise the bodies of Mary Rust and Jane Sinclair were likely to turn up in the Cherwell or the Isis, all the evidence against Vic and her friend would be destroyed, and there would be no hope of bringing them to justice until—

Until, Tansey thought, in a month, six months, a year they recommenced their obscene operations. Because it was Tansey's belief, and he had been proved right time after time, that once people like Vic had tasted unlimited power over their fellow-creatures, they yearned to repeat the experience. Which was why they had to be found and charged, and brought to justice.

Back in his office Chief Inspector Tansey telephoned the hospital and spoke to the consultant in charge of Linda

Jackson. She was still unconscious, but her condition was said to be improved and the prognosis was more hopeful. From time to time she muttered, though so far it had been impossible for the police officer sitting beside her—or anyone else—to distinguish any meaningful words.

It seemed there was no immediate likelihood that this situation would change. Indeed, the consultant warned Tansey that there might be a sudden deterioration in the patient's condition, and it was still not inconceivable that she might die without regaining consciousness.

Depressed at this news, the Chief Inspector then telephoned Mrs Mercer, who sounded none too pleased to hear from him so soon. Her mother, she said, had been very upset the previous evening and had not yet recovered; she would be spending the day in bed, and in no circumstances could she be questioned further. However, Mrs Mercer had again asked her about Vic's second name, as the Chief Inspector had said it was important, and Mrs Stein had agreed that after all it might be Brown or Browne, which, according to the daughter, just showed how confused her mother was.

Tansey thanked Mrs Mercer, and sat for a minute staring at his phone, wondering what steps to take next. Ideally, what he needed was some definite identification of Vic, which would satisfy him—if not the Chief Constable—and he wanted it quickly, before rumours that Linda Jackson was alive started to seep out to the media. Given any such identification—or even anything pointing towards it—he would act himself—and to hell with the consequences.

He tapped out Mrs Wadham's number. Mrs Wadham was ready to help, but doubted her ability to do so. She had not known Vic well. She hadn't seen Vic for a year or more. She couldn't guarantee to recognize Vic in different clothes, a different hair-style, perhaps a hat. And what was more, she claimed that from a legal point of view she would be a worthless witness.

'Any barrister would make a mockery of my evidence,

Chief Inspector,' she said. 'You see, I'm a wee bit vain. I should wear spectacles, but I don't, and I've never managed those contact lenses. So, unless I'm by myself, doing accounts or reading or watching the box, I'm afraid I don't see other people's faces as clearly as I might.'

Obviously, the fates were not on his side, Tansey decided as he replaced his receiver. But he had to take some action. He couldn't just wait until Rust and Sinclair were destroyed, or Vic abducted another girl to replace Linda Jackson. Better to take a risk. He couldn't literally defy the Chief Constable, but—A plan was beginning to form in his mind. It was hazardous, in a sense, and he couldn't involve any of his colleagues, though he supposed he must take Sergeant Greenway into his confidence. But it was the only way forward that he could see.

'You're crazy,' Hilary Greenway exclaimed.

'Okay, I'm crazy. But no one's asking you to share in my craziness,' said Tansey. 'As a matter of courtesy I told you what I intended, and if you're determined to push your elegant little nose in where it's not wanted—'

'It may not be wanted, but it's needed. If you're going to do this off the record, you need all the trained help you can get. It will reduce the risk, if nothing else. You can't operate with just an amateur.'

'But your presence will make it more official, don't forget. My shopping in the middle of the day when I ought to be working could be a nice coincidence—but not two of us. Or am I meant to be there to carry your groceries— Sergeant?'

'To hell with you—sir!'

Two bright spots of colour flared in Hilary Greenway's cheeks. She glared at Tansey, who regarded her with an ever-widening smile. She stopped the car with a jerk in front of the pub where they were to meet Peter Cousin. She was furious, and Tansey was thrown forward on to his seat-belt.

'That,' he said mildly, 'is our first quarrel,' and he laughed as if he were enormously pleased.

'Look,' he went on, 'if things go wrong, I shall have put up a very large black. If they go badly wrong, I could be back on the beat. I don't want that to happen to you.'

'Why not? In a way it's my case as much as yours, and I've as much right as you have to—to be crazy. Haven't I?'

'All right. I suppose so.' Tansey capitulated. 'Okay. We're in it together, assuming that Peter Cousin is prepared to play. We need someone who won't be recognized, and I can't think of anyone else. Besides, if he really was in love with Kate, he has a motive for helping us. Let's go in, and see what he says.'

Peter Cousin was sitting in a corner of the bar, morosely surveying half a pint of bitter. He had been surprised when the Chief Inspector had asked to meet him that evening for a quiet off the record chat, but he had agreed. The sight of Greenway failed to cheer him. If the Sergeant were to be present the 'chat' would more likely be an interrogation.

'Well, what is it now?' he said, brushing aside Tansey's apologies for their lateness. 'I imagine you're not going to arrest me, not over a beer?'

'That's far from our intention,' said Tansey. 'On the contrary, I'm hoping you'll help us to arrest the people who caused Kate Minden's death.'

'You don't mean it! You know?' Cousin stared at him.

'Let me get us some drinks, and I'll explain. The other half for you? Or would you prefer something short?'

'Gin and bitter lemon, please, if it's coming out of the police budget,' said Cousin, his face still mirroring disbelief.

'It's not,' retorted Tansey, as he went towards the bar, 'but you're welcome, nevertheless.'

'Now,' he said, returning with the drinks. 'We know— that's to say, I know and Sergeant Greenway knows—but our Chief Constable won't act without more evidence. We intend to get that evidence, and you could help us.'

'Manufacture it, do you mean?'

'No, I do not,' Tansey said firmly. 'Let me explain what we'd like you to do, and why. Then you can decide if you're prepared to cooperate. Needless to say, there's absolutely no compulsion. All we ask is, if you want no part in it, just forget we've ever had this conversation.'

'Of course,' Cousin said. 'But I can tell you right now that if I can help in any way to put the blasted shit who did those unspeakable things to Kate behind bars for the next twenty years, I'm on.'

'All right,' said Tansey. 'Then listen.'

Peter Cousin listened. The ice melted in his drink, but he failed to notice. He kept his eyes on Tansey's face, and nodded from time to time in understanding. His expression was grim as Tansey stopped speaking.

'Not only will I do what you want,' he said, 'but I'll do it with the utmost pleasure.'

'It may involve hanging around for a day or two, waiting for an opportunity which may never come, and in the meantime you'll be missing business,' Tansey warned.

'Too bad!' Cousin shrugged and, suddenly realizing that there was a glass in front of him, he took a deep drink. 'Luckily Tony Knight's an accommodating kind of bloke, and I'll make it up to him afterwards.'

'There's also the possibility that we're wrong,' Tansey pointed out.

'But you don't believe you are?' Cousin looked from Tansey to Greenway.

'No,' they said in unison.

'Then that settles it.' Unexpectedly Peter Cousin grinned. 'Right or wrong, I shall plead accident. In the unlikely event I'm charged with assault and found guilty it'll be a first offence, and I should get off with a fine. I'll expect you to pay it, Chief Inspector. All I hope is that you find this Vic. I'd gladly go to prison myself if it would help you do that,' he added seriously.

*

They sat in the unmarked police car and watched the tall grey brick house on the other side of the road. They had spent most of the previous day there and, apart from the milkman and the postman, no one had come or gone.

'Lord, I hope something happens soon,' Peter Cousin said.

'Me too,' said Sergeant Greenway.

They had run out of conversation, and she could think of nothing else to say. She shared his impatience. It was boring work, sitting and watching and waiting—keeping 'obbo', as they used to call it in her early days on the force—never able to relax completely, because swift decisive action might be required at any moment.

Suddenly she stiffened. The car window was slightly open, and she had heard a door slam. A minute later first a wheel and then a whole bicycle appeared, carried by Dr Paul Avery up the basement steps of the house opposite. At the same time the front door opened and Miss Gower, watering can in hand, came out on to the steps to attend to her plants.

'That's Avery, the doctor, who lives with Linda Jackson,' Greenway explained hurriedly. 'He must have spent the night there. The woman is Miss Gower.'

'That white-haired old lady?' said Cousin incredulously.

'She's not so old. Fifty-odd,' Greenway said, and caught her breath. 'Oh God, I hope he's not telling her. We warned him no one was to know that Linda was alive, but—'

Leaning on his bicycle, Paul Avery seemed to be holding a lengthy conversation with Miss Gower. Then he waved a hand, mounted his bike and rode down the short drive to the street. Miss Gower began to water the flowers, and Sergeant Greenway heaved a sigh of relief.

'Crisis over, I think,' she said.

She had spoken too soon. Almost immediately the garage door opened, and a blue Ford Escort was backed out, slowly but efficiently. It turned in the narrow space available, and headed for the street. Sergeant Greenway was already on the radio to Chief Inspector Tansey at Headquarters.

CHAPTER 20

'We're heading north, sir. With any luck towards that big supermarket on the Northampton road. I suggest you make in that direction.'

'Right, Sergeant. I'm on my way.'

The Chief Inspector sounded out of breath. On his receipt of Greenway's first call, he had raced down the corridor, to the surprise of several junior officers who had impeded him, and hurled himself into his car. Now he started the engine and drove dangerously fast out of the parking lot.

The radio messages continued, culminating in, 'As I thought, we're at the supermarket, sir. Cousin's just following her in. I'll wait for you at the main entrance.'

And ten minutes later Sergeant Greenway was joined by the Chief Inspector. Together they went through the large glass doors, which opened smoothly and silently at their approach, and entered the huge store. At this hour of the morning trade was moderately brisk. Naturally, most of the shoppers were women, many of them with children, and Tansey felt a little conspicuous until Greenway picked up a basket, tossed one or two articles into it and handed it to him.

'There they are!' she said. 'By the cheese counter, but there are too many people about near there. He'll have to wait, choose his moment.'

'We've got to keep him in sight.'

Leaving Greenway to follow him, Tansey hurried down an aisle, only to find himself faced by two women, gossiping happily while their combined trolleys blocked the passage.

He pushed past them roughly, letting his sergeant make the necessary apologies and, momentarily thwarted by another woman with a couple of small children, bit back a curse. Then, rounding a corner, he was in time to witness a scene, extraordinary in this or any other supermarket.

It was intended to look like an accident, but it could readily be interpreted for what it really was—a planned, unprovoked attack on a middle-aged woman, peacefully doing her shopping.

For, seizing his opportunity when there were no young children or elderly couples nearby, when no one was observing events closely and when Miss Foyne was reaching up to take a can of peaches from a top shelf, Cousin had rammed the trolley that he'd been pushing since he entered the supermarket into the small of her back. Miss Foyne cried out with pain and, as Cousin released the trolley's pressure, stumbled backwards and fell to the ground, bringing with her a cascade of canned fruit and vegetables.

The noise was appalling, and brought an almost immediate response from staff and customers. Some who merely saw the end of the attack took it at its face value as an accident but, especially in view of what happened next, some thought the man had gone mad. In fact, Peter Cousin had never been more sane.

Although the incident had happened without warning and had taken Miss Foyne by surprise, her reactions were immediate. With one hand firmly plonked on her hat she was already struggling to her feet as store assistants and customers came running to help. Some other shoppers merely stood and stared, the Chief Inspector and Sergeant Greenway among them. At first sight their plan, it seemed, had failed.

But they had underrated Peter Cousin. If he had had any doubts before at the sight of this apparently respectable woman, they vanished as she instinctively used a hand to protect her hat rather than help to break her fall. He flung himself on her to prevent her from rising, and they struggled fiercely together while the bystanders watched, astounded. It was some seconds before a few people recovered their wits, and made efforts to prise Cousin away.

They succeeded at last, and Cousin was pulled free. Miss Foyne's hat was lying on the floor among the canned goods, but Cousin held aloft a wig of short grey hair. And Miss Foyne's head was seen by all to be completely bald, and smooth as a baby's bottom—just as her late employer, David Stein, had described it.

'Give it me! Give it back to me!' she screamed, reaching for her wig.

Cousin paid her no attention, and she raked his cheek with her nails before she seized her hat from the floor and jammed it down on her head. By now the supermarket manager had arrived on the scene, and an altercation began. At this, Tansey and Greenway decided it was time to intervene.

Tansey said formally, producing his warrant card, 'I am a police officer—Detective Chief Inspector Tansey—and my sergeant here and I witnessed this incident. I think you had both better come with us.'

Miss Foyne had recovered herself sufficiently to protest at once. 'Me? Come with you? What for? What have *I* done?' she demanded. 'This man attacked me. Ask anyone. They saw what happened. You said you saw it yourself. He assaulted me and—and shamed me in front of everyone.'

At last Tansey had got what he wanted, additional evidence that Miss Foyne was Vic. It was not totally conclusive, of course, but it was adequate for his purposes. He would not be deterred now. 'In that case we shall need you as a witness,' he said firmly. 'And I think it would be better if you both came to Headquarters.'

He turned to the supermarket manager and drew him aside. The manager nodded, and began, with the help of his staff, to clear a way through the crowd.

'But it wasn't her fault,' one of the shoppers called out. 'I saw it all. It was him. He's a raving maniac, if you ask me. He wanted her wig, he did.'

There was a murmur of agreement from the mainly female crowd, eager to defend one of their own sex against an aggressive male. Peter Cousin glared at them, but he was essentially a mild and private man, and he was beginning to be horrified at the situation he had created. Tansey began to fear there might be real trouble, but the efforts of the supermarket's staff were having their effect in calming the customers.

'Come along then, madam,' Greenway said gently. 'And we'll sort this out at Headquarters.'

Miss Foyne continued to protest in a shocked lady-like way, but she made no further attempt to resist. Her eyes, however, were like hard brown pebbles, and the sergeant could feel the hatred exuding from her.

Tansey had a few further words with the supermarket manager who, as a matter of form, began to take the names and addresses of those who had witnessed the whole scene, and within minutes the Chief Inspector found himself sitting beside Miss Foyne in the rear of the police car, and being driven by Sergeant Greenway to Headquarters. He had tossed the keys of the car in which he himself had reached the supermarket to Peter Cousin, who was following them in convoy. Miss Foyne's car, the blue Ford Escort, would have to be collected later, he thought, and examined by the experts in an effort to find traces of the abducted girls.

'Hurry, Sergeant! Hurry,' he said.

'Yes, Sergeant, hurry,' echoed Miss Foyne. 'The sooner we get somewhere where I can speak to someone in authority and deal with this disgraceful business, the better. You're going to regret what you've done to me today, Chief Inspector, I promise you.'

'We'll see, madam.'

Tansey was non-committal. He had got Foyne under

control, and his main object was to keep her out of circulation for an hour or two—if not considerably longer. She must have no opportunity to warn Miss Gower, nor must Miss Gower be alarmed by the prolonged absence of her friend. He didn't intend to allow Gower to barricade herself in her house, and take a last-minute revenge on Mary Rust and Jane Sinclair—assuming they were both still alive.

'Sergeant, get on the phone,' he said. 'I want an inspector and a WPC to meet us in the entrance hall to take charge of this lady. She's to be put in an interrogation room, and is not to be allowed to communicate with anyone—and I mean anyone, even if she swears she's the Chief Constable's sister. Serious charges are expected to be preferred later.'

These instructions gave rise to another outburst from Miss Foyne. 'What serious charges?' she demanded at once. 'And why am I being treated like this? And where's that wretched young man who attacked me?'

Tansey ignored her and she relapsed into silence for the rest of the journey—itself perhaps a pointer to a guilty conscience, the Chief Inspector reflected, as they reached their Headquarters. Miss Foyne's transfer to the care of a somewhat surprised inspector and WPC, who had been expecting a dangerous criminal, was made peacefully. Tansey gave instructions about the Ford Escort, and warned, 'Don't be taken in by her appearance. She is *not* a nice harmless lady.' He was outside again in minutes.

Sergeant Greenway was talking to Peter Cousin. 'I've been saying how grateful we are,' she reported to the Chief Inspector. 'Mr Cousin was wonderful, wasn't he?'

'He was indeed,' Tansey agreed. 'I can't thank you enough.'

'There's no need for thanks,' Cousin said. 'I hope she gets life. That is if—if it's proved. You know, driving here I was suddenly scared. After all, she can't be the only middle-aged woman in the district wearing a wig. If she'd had an illness

or treatment for cancer she could have lost her hair and—
and . . . It would be ghastly if . . .'

'We'll know in half an hour or less.' Tansey was brusque.
'And if I'm wrong it will, as you say, be ghastly. But I don't
believe I am.'

'Where are you going? To arrest the other one, the one
who was watering her plants?' All Cousin's doubts seemed
to have returned.

'That's exactly what we're going to try to do right now
—and you're holding us up, Mr Cousin.'

'Can I come with you?' Cousin said suddenly.

The Chief Inspector hesitated. It was not against regu-
lations, and in any case he had already bent the rules
completely out of shape that morning. 'Why not?' he said.
'But let's get going.'

Miss Gower was peering anxiously out of one of her front
windows when they drew up before the house. Tansey had
feared that she might make difficulties and refuse to let them
in, but when he introduced himself, she opened the door
wide.

'Yes, I remember. I saw you with Dr Avery, and this
young lady came in to use the telephone once.' Miss Gower
glanced at Cousin, but didn't comment on his presence. 'What is it you want? Is it about poor Linda? More
inquiries?'

'It's more inquiries, yes, Miss Gower.'

'Oh! Come on in, then. I—I was afraid. Perhaps an
accident. My friend, Miss Foyne, went shopping, and she's
been gone such a long time.'

'The traffic is very bad today,' Sergeant Greenway volunteered.

'Is it, dear? That explains it then.'

Miss Gower led the way into the large sitting-room which
stretched across the rear of the house. Here they seemed to
be one floor up, as the flat in the basement below was, at

the back, on a level with the garden. Peter Cousin went and stared out of the window, as though distancing himself from what he feared was to happen. But Miss Gower seemed quite unaware—and unafraid.

'Now, what is it?' she said. 'How can I help you?'

'We wish to search the house,' Tansey said bluntly.

'Search the house? This house? Why ever should you want to do that?' Miss Gower's reaction was natural enough, but to Tansey, watching her closely, she seemed to have suddenly become tense. 'Anyway, I don't think I can let you, not until Miss Foyne returns, at least. It's her house, you know, not mine.'

'I must insist, Miss Gower.'

'But you can't. You have no right,' she objected. 'Shouldn't you have a—a search warrant, don't you call it?'

'Miss Gower, I propose to go through this house.' Tansey was quite aware he was exceeding his authority, but he swept aside the woman's protests. He had no intention of retreating at this stage. 'Will you show me around, or will you stay here with Sergeant Greenway?'

'I—I—Oh, very well, Chief Inspector. Come with me.'

Her face scarlet under her fluffy white hair, Miss Gower marched out of the room, her short, squat figure exuding righteous indignation. Tansey kept very close to her, followed by Greenway and a slightly reluctant Cousin. It was a large house, and Miss Gower showed them everything, even the larder and the toilet in the back hall, and the space under the stairs. As they progressed upwards, she flung open cupboard doors and displayed the contents of wardrobes.

'I don't know what you're looking for, Chief Inspector, but you're not going to find it here,' she said angrily.

Watching her thick legs as she climbed the last flight of stairs that led to the attics, Tansey, behind her, was inclined to agree. He had been wrong. He'd blown it. He'd jumped to conclusions. It was obvious that the girls weren't here. And he hadn't so much as seen a camera—the kind of

everyday object one would expect to find in any house—or
even a roll of film.

The attic rooms were carpeted and sparsely furnished.
Dejected and resigned, the Chief Inspector dutifully glanced
around as Miss Gower opened a cupboard in the first attic,
and disdainfully suggested by a wave of her stubby hand
that he look under the bed. They went through the same
performance in the next room.

'These rooms aren't used,' Miss Gower said unnecessarily, 'but Miss Foyne and I keep our winter clothes in the
cupboards and wardrobes.'

'Yes, so I see,' said Tansey. He turned to go; all he wanted
to do now was escape from the house.

But Miss Gower had no intention of letting him off so
lightly. 'Well,' she said, 'I hope you and your—your friends
are satisfied, Chief Inspector.'

'No!'

Surprisingly it was Peter Cousin who had spoken. No one
had been paying him any attention, and he had been staring
out of a window and glancing around the place as if
thoroughly bored, or perhaps embarrassed. Now both
Sergeant Greenway and Miss Gower turned to him. The
Chief Inspector, however, kept his eyes on Miss Gower's
face, and he saw her expression change from triumph to
something approximating fear.

'What—what do you mean?' she said.

Cousin addressed Tansey. 'There must be another room
up here,' he said, 'long and narrow, behind these two. You
can tell from the shape of the house, or I can. After all, it's
my job. I know about houses. It's my business.'

'But where—' Tansey began. Then, 'Of course. One of
the cupboards.'

He thrust Miss Gower out of the way, pushed aside the
heavy winter coats and garment bags, and at once saw the
outline of a door. There was no key, nor any keyhole, but
what at first appeared to be a hook in the middle twisted,

and almost the whole back of the cupboard opened. He stepped through into the long, narrow room that Cousin had predicted.

There were three mattresses on the floor. He recognized Jane Sinclair and Mary Rust. They were covered with duvets, and lying deeply asleep, obviously drugged. The third mattress was empty and, it seemed to Tansey, ominously waiting for an occupant. Except for a covered bucket in a corner, there was no other furniture.

A door at the end of the room was locked, and he guessed it led to another room, presumably the photographic studio. He didn't bother with it for the moment. The girls were of prime importance.

'Thank God, they're alive,' Greenway was saying, on her knees beside them.

'And thank friend Cousin here too,' said Tansey. 'Bring her along!' He pointed to Miss Gower who, not made of such stern stuff as Miss Foyne, had collapsed on the floor and was rocking herself backwards and forwards, moaning gently.

He ran downstairs ahead of them. It was urgent to get to a phone. The first priority was an ambulance. Then, when the girls were safe, the police could go into action, the experts could move in and the case—or cases—against Vic and her companion could be substantiated.

'But all that leaves one question,' said Hilary Greenway, when they were at last alone. 'Motive.'

'Motive! We hardly need it, now we've caught them in the act, as it were—red-handed, as they used to say. But think what the media will make of it. Two unattractive frustrated middle-aged women. Sex must have been the motivating force—'

'And pornography is sex at a distance, if you like,' interrupted Greenway. 'It's production gave them power of a kind over women—their models, the beautiful girls they envied so much—and over men, too, in a sense.'

'You know the words, Hilary,' Tansey hesitated; it was the first time he had ever used her first name. Then he went on, ' "Inhibited sexuality"—that's the phrase. It's in the popular press once a week, nowadays.'

'Yes,' said Hilary Greenway, 'I know the words.'

CHAPTER 21

The three girls recovered completely. Jane Sinclair, who had been held the shortest time, was the first to return home to her husband and child. Then Mary Rust, whose parents were selling up their shop and leaving Colombury, was collected from hospital by Brian Quayle, whom she was to marry. And eventually Linda Avery rejoined her husband.

As soon as they were able, the girls talked—and they had learnt a lot, in spite of the sedation they had suffered, but they were vague about details many of which emerged during interrogation of the two women. Most of Chief Inspector Tansey's and Sergeant Greenway's surmises and conjectures were proved accurate. Miss Foyne was clearly the leader of the pair. She had seemingly conceived a hatred for men—and for beautiful women—early in life. She had been born ugly, and her parents had made no secret of their disgust. The last straw had been to lose her hair thanks to a childhood illness. She had come to regard her wig as a symbol of sexual incompetence. Eventually over the years, her fetishes had hardened; hair was one, beauty another.

She had trained as a photographer—after all, photographers exercise an element of control over their subjects —and had eventually joined forces in Reading with Miss Gower, another acidulated spinster. Their precise relationship was never clearly defined, but once Miss Foyne had inherited the Oxford house and its facilities, together they had decided to demonstrate their place—their power—in a seemingly hostile world by a series of abductions of beautiful girls—and the publication of their photographs in obscene poses in pornographic magazines.

The girls who survived made the technique clear. Kidnapping and threats and sedation—with major tranquillizers, as the pathologist had suggested and as had been confirmed by the PM on Kate Minden. Apparently the two accused women had without any trouble acquired from their respective Health Service and private doctors sufficient prescriptions for these drugs to assemble a considerable supply; after all, the symptoms to present were easy enough to fake: anxiety, insomnia, aches and pains apparently unrelated to any organic condition. And then the photography. In many senses, the girls had no idea precisely what they were involved in; certainly they had no thoughts that the pictures might be published.

All that Mary Rust, the brunette, and Linda, the blonde, knew of Kate Minden's death were sounds of a struggle from the studio next to their room, the noise of what might have been a floodlight crashing to the ground, followed by an agonizing scream. Later that night a covered figure had been carried into the corridor. This had been enough to reduce the remaining two girls to acquiescence, though Linda Jackson had later attempted to escape by taking an overdose of the sedative that was being administered to them. As far as Mary and Jane Sinclair, the red-headed replacement for Kate who had by then joined the group, were concerned, Linda had then been carted off to an uncertain fate.

The keys to the choice of victims were of course beauty and hair colour. None of the kidnappings had been entirely fortuitous; the women had meticulously searched for the ideal models, studied their movements and seized opportunities. Kate they had seen in the Kidlington office, and had become aware of her Abingdon life. Admittedly it was by chance that they were following Mary when she made her excursion into Copley Woods with Brian Quayle, but she in her distress had been grateful, like Kate before her, to accept a lift from two seemingly harmless older women. Linda Jackson was naturally well-known to them, and Jane Sinclair's travels followed a regular pattern. The two kidnappers had made their plans and carried them out carefully and efficiently, thought Tansey and Greenway—and the Judge and jury.

Margaret Victoria Foyne and Dorothy Stella Gower were both found guilty of abduction, manslaughter and attempted murder. The question of Gus Hunter's murder had been raised, but the Director of Public Prosecutions had ruled that the evidence for this crime was insufficient. He had also decided that a prosecution under some obscenity law would merely make a media holiday.

To Tansey's fury, they both successfully pleaded insanity, but they were sentenced to be detained at Her Majesty's pleasure; as Hilary Greenway pointed out, the full details of the case would be available to any psychiatric or parole board, so that, in view of their ages, this should be quite sufficient.

As for Detective Chief Inspector Tansey and Detective-Sergeant Greenway, they were commended by the Chief Constable. He was a sensible man, and generous with his praise.

Hilary and Dick celebrated—so far as such an appalling case could be celebrated—by dining together again.

It was, they found to their surprise, a slightly embarrassing occasion. It took place at the Randolph Hotel in Oxford, and their conversation was at first stilted—and ridden with 'shop'.

However, as the evening progressed, with drinks and wine and, later, brandy and a liqueur, their talk became steadily more intimate.

Eventually, Dick Tansey said, 'Oh hell, Hilary, enough of this nonsense. You know what I want to say. We both know the words.'

Hilary stared at him, and grinned. 'Yes, Dick,' she said, 'I certainly know the words. But this time you must say them.'